Marilyn Holdeman
301 Crescent St.
Goshen, Indiana

This Way Out

OTHER BOOKS BY PAUL HUTCHENS

**In Our $1.25 Christian
Fiction Series for Adults**

ROMANCE OF FIRE
THIS WAY OUT
THE VISION
SHAFTED SUNLIGHT
BLAZE STAR
MASTERING MARCUS
THE LAST FIRST
WINDBLOWN
THIS IS LIFE
A SONG FOREVER
THE VOICE
YESTERDAY'S RAIN
CUP OF COLD WATER
ECLIPSE
MORNING FLIGHT

For Children 8-14 Years Old:

THE SUGAR CREEK GANG
WE KILLED A BEAR
FURTHER ADVENTURES OF THE SUGAR CREEK GANG
THE SUGAR CREEK GANG GOES CAMPING
THE SUGAR CREEK GANG IN CHICAGO
THE SUGAR CREEK GANG IN SCHOOL
MYSTERY AT SUGAR CREEK
THE SUGAR CREEK GANG FLIES TO CUBA

This Way Out

by

PAUL HUTCHENS

SEVENTH EDITION

WM. B. EERDMANS PUBLISHING COMPANY

Grand Rapids   1942   Michigan

First Printing, September, 1935
Second Printing, December, 1935
Third Printing, September, 1937
Fourth Printing, February, 1938
Fifth Printing, November, 1938
Sixth Printing, January, 1942

PRINTED IN THE UNITED STATES OF AMERICA

This Way Out

CHAPTER I

James Fownley slowly closed the door of his room, waited for the sound of the clicking of the latch, turned the key in the lock, snapped on the lights and faced about nervously.

"I'll do it tonight," he muttered to himself.

Slowly, carefully, as if being impelled, he walked to the window, closed and locked it and drew the shade.

Again his eyes circled the room. They came to focus on the full length mirror before him. For only a brief moment he stared at the man within. "Jim," he said, "take a good look at yourself —for the last time."

The discouraged dark eyes softened while his hands fumbled for his pocket comb. A stray lock of brown hair had dropped to his temple from an otherwise perfectly groomed head. As if in indecision he adjusted his tie, flicked a particle of dust from the lapel of his coat and toyed briefly with his watch-chain.

From the mirror he made his way to the writing desk at the far side of the room, near the window. There he sat down. His hand was steady as it reached out to clasp, firmly, almost tenderly, a small gilt-edged picture frame from which the picture itself had been removed. Shattered glass lay scattered over the top of the desk. With a blotter he cleared a space.

Then, still slowly, he lifted a waste-basket from the floor and emptied its contents on the desk. His fingers began to unfold, meticulously, the one piece of crumpled paper which had been the sole contents of the wastebasket.

"For the last time." The words came with hesitation. Yet his movements were exact and — as the heavy paper was smoothed out — almost caressing.

"How beautiful she is. And how false." He thought again of the terrible moment when he had discovered how false she was.

The rhythmic ticking of the clock on the shelf above came to his ears with new meaning as it re-echoed the thoughts of his mind: "Un-true, un-true, un-true."

7

"But you will never again have a chance," he said, grimly. His jaw set, his eyes took on a fixed stare. He rose to his feet. "Not only 'tonight' but now — *now!*"

Seizing his pen he wrote briefly across the back of the photograph:

"Faithless Marlyn:
"Had you told me the truth, had you never told me you cared for me, I might have forgiven you, but now I cannot. Like Launcelot, your faith has been unfaithful and you have been only falsely true. I cannot stand the pain of it, so I take this way out. Does any man know a better way?
"James."

He laid aside the pen and crossed once more to his mirror. This time there was no smile, and his eyes were determined. He must hurry. A haunting, driving mania seized him. He sprang to his feet, rushed to the bureau, and searched its drawers. "Ah!" he gasped, the gasp a curious paradox of satisfaction and terror.

"Hello, James!" a woman's musical voice sounded behind him.

He turned. "Marlyn! What in the — where did you come from?"

"Out of the sky," was the reply, "from which all evil angels fall."

He moved toward her, his hands clenched, every muscle tense, the gun still held in his right hand. "Fallen angels should be in ——" He leveled the gun at her.

"Oh no, they shouldn't. At least not this one. And not now. Your gun is empty, James, and there is no ammunition in the room. I saw to that. I was afraid you'd try something rash, after — *that.*" She motioned toward the desk.

His eyes followed hers as he tossed the revolver onto the bed. "Yes," he said savagely, "and if you'd been here at that time I'd have ——"

"I *was* here."

"You ——"

"Angels have a way, you know."

He stared at her fixedly. The awful strain of the past days since he had discovered her faithlessness had risen higher and higher in its intensity until it had driven him to the climactic desire to find "a way out." It brought him now to complete exhaustion. He sank into the arms of a deeply cushioned chair where he relaxed, his eyes still upon her.

"You're tired, Jimmy," she said, her voice suddenly softening. "Jimmy," was the name she had used when she had promised to marry him, the name she had always used when she had told him of her love. Those were the days when she *had* been an angel to him, and when he had loved her with a flaming, unquenchable love, until it seemed he could not live without her. And she had set their wedding day.

This was to have been the day. But — Warburne! Tall, dark, perfectly groomed, suave — and a way with women. Two months ago she had met him, had become secretly infatuated with him, forgotten everything else. No wonder "Jimmy" had become "James."

"Tired, sick, and everything else, but not 'Jimmy,'" he returned.

She reached for a cigarette. She knew he hated that. He had hoped it would be a passing whim, but it had stuck, as Warburne had.

Coolly she stood there before him, tall, gorgeous, faintly wreathed in smoke. Only Marlyn could look like that. She needed not the embellishments of tonight's jaunty black frock and cape to make her beautiful. Marlyn was always ravishing, even when she was stabbing him to the very heart with things she did and said. Her arrows, barbed with beauty and charm, were only the more painful.

At length she spoke, the smoke making a halo of blue about her head, "Not 'Jimmy'?"

"Not now, nor ever!"

She watched him pensively, calmly aware that she was moving him, that her very presence was binding up the wounds she had made. She had lost him, temporarily, but she could win him back. He would be at her feet in a moment, as so often before.

"And why?" she persisted.

He did not reply.

"And why not 'Jimmy'?"

He was still silent while he toyed with his watch chain. Then he looked up. "Today is the twentieth." His eyes turned to the calendar over the fireplace.

She followed his gaze, then lifted her wrist-watch to her vision. "And it is not yet midnight."

She crossed to his chair, flicking the cigarette stub into the fireplace. She saw his hands tremble as she approached. "Jimmy!"

He stiffened, and turned his face away.

"Jimmy." Her voice was crooning and soft, "Is — is it too late? Can't we — ?"

"You know it's too late," he said. It was evident he was speaking with considerable effort. But he began again. "Warburne —"

"It was a mistake, Jimmy," she cried. "It was you all the time. I know that now. I was wrong, Jimmy."

"What happened to Warburne? Where is he now? Are you tired of him already?"

"He's dead," she announced.

He started and turned to face her.

"Two days ago," she said. "His sailboat was sunk off the coast. Didn't you see it in the papers?"

"So that's it!" he returned savagely. "That is like you. You had better have been on the boat with him. Warburne is dead, and now you come whimpering back to me. Your treasure house is exhausted, your toy balloon is punctured, you tire of the far country and the husks and you come back to me! Well, you can find another Warburne." He reached for his hat and started toward the door.

But she was there before him. "Jimmy, O Jimmy!" she cried. "I didn't love him! I only thought I did! It's you, only you! Can't you forgive me?" She threw herself upon him, burying her face against his shoulder.

But he stood there, cold and unresponsive. "You've played with me enough. You don't know what love is. All you want is another plaything. There will be plenty of them. Go find someone else." He thrust her from him, unlocked the door and stepped out.

CHAPTER II

The Walhurst was a hotel catering largely to the middle class. At this hour of the night, Fallenby would be at the desk. Fallenby was tall, lanky, slow thinking, good-natured, in his early twenties. He nodded as James approached.

"Going out again?"

"To stay," Fownley answered. "How much do I owe?"

"To stay? Say, now, that's too —"

"I say, how much do I owe?"

Fallenby looked at his questioner and something he saw moved him to immediate action. "Just a minute." His lanky frame unfolded and he began to turn the pages of the desk record. "The book shows thirty-five dollars, including the rest of this week."

Fownley tossed over two twenty dollar bills. "Keep the tip."

"Thanks, a lot. Anything wrong? — I mean, you're not sick or anything?"

Fownley ignored the question. "I'm leaving my suit-case and a few belongings. If I'm not back by Saturday, they're yours."

"Say, Mr. Fownley, that's sure swell of you."

Again Fownley brushed him aside. "Answer this question, will you? Who let that woman into my room?"

Giles started and glanced about. "Why, what's wrong?"

"Why did you let her in?"

"I didn't let anyone into your room. There was a woman here who wanted 306, the room next to yours. She said she always has it when she stays here."

"And you let her have it! But how did she get into my room?"

"I can't imagine. Maybe she bribed a chambermaid. They're not incorruptible, you know. Maybe she went through the keyhole." Seeing that his pleasantry was not very well received, he went on. "I'm very sorry that such a thing should have happened. We'll have her changed right away, sir."

11

Fownley looked at him silently across the desk, saw the uselessness of saying anything more sharp than "All right," and then turned toward the door.

He entered the street, his hat pulled down over his eyes. The events of the past hour flashed across his mind in kaleidoscopic pictures. This was to have been their wedding day. For a moment he sought to convince himself it was all a mistake; that Warburne had never come; that Marlyn had remained the same sweet, wonderful girl he had thought her to be.

Perhaps it was not yet too late. Maybe she had told the truth when she said she loved him. If only he — He could yet change his mind. It would be simple. The marriage license was still in his pocket, had been ever since that day when they had gone together to the city clerk.

He stopped still. A stiff breeze was blowing. Flying clouds overhead raced swiftly before a driving wind. He would find a minister somewhere, and it could all be settled tonight.

But with the thought came a feeling of revulsion and there swept over him once again that same dull, sickening sensation that had come to him in his room. She had deceived him, lied to him, only pretended to love him, and then had cast him aside for Warburne. He shook himself. "I hate her!" he cried under his breath. "She is painted, beautiful — and *false*."

He hired a cab and drove to the bay. Here the waves rolled and tossed, lashed by the wild fury of the wind. "A bad night for anyone to be out," he thought. Down the long pier, he hurried, one mad desire still holding him, driving him to seek oblivion, forgetfulness of pain.

What was that? Voices from the end of the pier! A crescent moon, sailing low, cast a silvery veil over everything. It appeared and reappeared from behind the swift-moving clouds. Now he could see the dim outlines of two persons ahead of him.

"Stop it, I tell you! Leave me alone!" It was a woman's voice, clear and high.

"Don't be a prude, I'm not goin' to hurt you!" a man's thick voice spoke in return, and laughed harshly. "If you're taking a walk alone y' ought to be glad of a lil' frien'ly comp'ny."

James quickened his steps, walking cautiously lest he be heard. The moon now was completely hidden behind a bank of clouds. He was angered in finding that he was not to be alone. Was there nowhere a place of seclusion where he could die without being seen?

Again he heard the woman's voice. "Let me alone! Let go of me!"

As James hurried forward, above the noise of the waves his ears caught the sound of shuffling feet. Just then the moon sailed out into the open and revealed the two forms swaying back and forth at the very end of the pier. Suddenly the man caught her up in his arms and hurled her out over the edge.

"Be 'n angel, then, if you want to!" he shouted drunkenly after her. And turning, he began to run.

James heard the sound of the stumbling feet, heard, too, the screams of the woman. He forgot himself and raced swiftly, almost savagely forward.

The two men were near each other now, and James with a fierce swing of his right arm, caught him on the jaw. "You — you drunken devil!" he thundered. His blow was well-placed and the man crumpled as he slipped and fell sprawling. For only a brief second James stood over him. The cries of the woman aroused him and he rushed to her rescue.

Now he could see her struggling with the waves. He threw off his coat and shoes and dived in.

It seemed an eternity before he had reached her and had fought his way back to the pier and climbed with her up the narrow stairway to the platform above. She was cold and trembling pitifully, but fully conscious. She tried to stand but could not, and staggered helplessly against him. He threw his topcoat about her. "Quick!" he said. "You must get home, and change those clothes."

"I — thank you so much. I can walk now, I think." But she crumpled in a heap at his feet.

"I'll carry you," he said. He drew on his shoes. The wind blew cold and harder than ever, it seemed, as he lifted her and started toward the street. Now they were at the place where the man had fallen. He was nowhere in sight. James stopped, his eyes searching the dark waters. The man had fallen in or else had hurried away like the coward that he was. James reflected, grimly, "If he has staggered into the water it is too late to help him now. Let him take my place. I am all out of the notion."

Somehow as he carried the girl down the long pier, he was glad that this had happened, glad that he was alive and that he had saved her.

As he neared the street the girl revived, and as they passed a light, opened her eyes. For a moment she struggled to free herself. "Let me go! Let me go! I —" Then she saw his face and was silent. "Forgive me," she said. "I forgot — I can walk now . . . please."

"You needn't," he said. He set her on her feet and steadied her as she reeled, then balanced herself.

"I'll call a cab," he told her, "and see you home."

"Oh, no — there isn't any home . . . not here."

"To your room, then."

"I'm stopping at the Walhurst."

"I'm staying there too. I'll take you there." He saw she was bewildered and as a cab passed, he hailed it.

"To the Walhurst," he announced, "and be quick!"

In the cab he pulled his coat about her snugly and watched her as she lay back against the corner. The light from the street allowed him to see her face. Pale, noticeably so because of her white skin, long, dark lashes, blue eyes, light brown hair, now hanging in a dishevelled mass on her shoulders, a firm chin. "Character," James thought. "A girl worth saving." Some girls were not.

He allowed himself to review in memory the scene at the pier. "Be an angel then!" That was what the man had said.

He looked at her again. "An angel! . . . I have rescued an angel . . . from death." . . . Someone else was to blame . . . But he had rescued her . . .Could there be any significance in his having saved this girl? Could he, perhaps . . . rescue Marlyn?

And he was still thinking about it as they drew up at the Walhurst.

"I'll be all right," the girl said, and thanked him again.

He touched his hat in acknowledgement of her appreciation. At the desk he said to Giles, after the girl had ascended in the elevator, "I've come back to change clothes."

"Miss Favis has taken another room," was Giles' reply. "Sorry about that."

"Forget it," James said, "and send up a half dozen towels."

Giles looked at him, wanting to ask as many questions. Where had Fownley been? What had happened? Why was the girl wearing his coat? But something in Fownley's eye kept him silent. "Yes, sir," he said. "Is that all?"

"That's all."

"A little whiskey? You're cold and —"

"Not for anything! I've seen too often what whiskey does. Good night."

In his room he hastily removed his wet garments and plunged into a hot bath. Twenty minutes later, wrapped in his bath robe he seated himself at his desk. Marlyn's picture was still there, lying face down. He lifted it but did not deign to turn it over, and, with his lips pressed firmly together, pushed it into a drawer. Then as if nothing unusual had happened in the past hours, he brushed the broken bits of glass into the waste basket. The picture frame he also placed in the drawer.

The gun was still lying on the bed when he went to retire. He picked it up, disinterestedly. "Hm! loaded! . . . That's strange." He walked to the bureau. An envelope was lying there. It said on the outside, "Mr. James Fownley." He recognized the handwriting as Marlyn's.

"I'm not interested," he told himself. Yet the eagerness with which he turned it over in his hands belied his words. He tore it open, unfolded the paper within, and read:

"Dear James:

"I have left your room just as it was — everything, even to the gun. I cannot believe you will do anything rash. You are too good to die. I regret deeply that I came to your room unwanted, but I am glad to have saved you, if only temporarily. Do not think you can ever escape me by taking your life; for the moment you do I shall follow you . . . even in death. If I could only be certain that I would really follow you. Is there anything after death, James? If I thought there was it might make a difference.

"Always yours,

"Marlyn."

He sat there with his eyes fixed upon the word "Marlyn." He had always liked the way she signed her name. There was something dainty about the characteristic flourishes, the way she made the "M" especially. He permitted himself to dream for a moment, even allowed himself to want her. But he brought his thoughts back to grim realities, and faced the truth. Marlyn was only trying to play on his emotions, even in her letter. Yet if the crisis ever came she would never keep her word, *even in death!*

"Even in death!" Was there anything after death? If so was it the same for all? There might be a chance for separation there. Perhaps she could not follow him. Did he want, really, to be away from her? . . . *eternally!* Vague memories of old theological truths, long ago discarded by him, came back to assert themselves, to insist on being heard . . . *"The wicked shall be turned into Hell," "The righteous shall go away into life eternal."*

He shrugged. It *would* make a difference, he admitted. But why a hell in the life to come when there was too much of it on earth now? He re-read the note, and reaching for his bill fold placed it therein. Might as well keep it.

There was a knock at the door. It was the elevator boy. "Your coat, sir," he said. "And here's a note."

James tipped the boy, hung the coat in the bath room, for it was still wet, and with strange emotion, scrutinized the white envelope. There was no name on the outside. Of course she did not know his name. He opened the envelope carefully, as if he were thinking of the girl herself and of the careful way in which he had carried her. She seemed so gentle, as if she could be so easily wounded . . . in spirit. Then he read:

"Mr. Rescuer:

"Thank you so very, very much for tonight, and for the coat. You have been so kind, I wish I might reward you in some special way. I would surely have drowned, for, although I can swim a little, the waves were too much for me.

"It was not because I was afraid to die, of that I am glad, for I was prepared. I know where I should have gone — to be with Christ.

"Again thanking you, I am,

"Yours very appreciatively,

"June Darle."

CHAPTER III

At a table in the far corner of the Walhurst dining room sat James Fownley. He had ordered a simple breakfast of poached eggs on toast with golden brown coffee. It was nine o'clock. He had slept well in spite of contrary anticipations.

A waiter sailed up. "Special edition of the morning paper," he announced, as he laid a copy of the paper beside James' plate. "Anything else?"

"Nothing, thanks — wait a minute, Grant. That book you wanted has come."

Grant beamed, broadly, showing his gleaming, white teeth. He liked Fownley; always had, since that day three months ago when Fownley had taken his first meal there and had left a dollar tip under the glass. And Fownley liked Grant; had found in him a companion. Grant hesitated before leaving. "Haven't had a streak of bad luck, or anything? You're eating alone, I see."

"And I'm going to stay that way, Grant."

Someone was entering the dining room. Fownley kept his eyes on the newspaper, scanning the columns for anything that might be of interest. He wanted to look up but feared lest the new arrival be Marlyn. If not Marlyn, then perhaps his new acquaintance, Miss Darle. He lifted the paper higher and buried his face behind it. When he did raise his eyes he took in his breath, sharply. June Darle was coming directly to his table.

"May I?" she asked as she touched the chair opposite him. There was not a vacant table in the entire dining room.

"Indeed, yes." He rose while Grant seated her, as only Grant Weston knew how.

"How courteous," she remarked to Fownley after Grant had left.

For only a second James appraised her, approving, highly, of her smartly simple black frock with a frilly white organdie collar.

"And extraordinarily intelligent," James replied, referring to Grant. "I've often wondered why he plays waiter. He could do something else and do it well."

"Most everyone could," she said, "you for instance."

"I could be a life guard, perhaps."

"Instead of?" The conversation was without strain.

"Managing a book store," he returned, easily. "And you?"

"Nothing, I wouldn't want to try anything else. I'm perfectly satisfied."

Her face was pale, as it had been last night, and without any make-up. Somehow she didn't need it. And she did look *satisfied*.

"You're a rare creature," he said, "if you are telling the truth."

"Oh, but I am!" she assured him.

Grant came and went and she looked with approval at what he had brought. "Excuse me a moment, please." She smiled across the table and bowed her head, silently. No words escaped her lips, but a thousand thoughts went racing through Fownley's brain. Who was this simple, lovely girl? She was not a girl, but a woman with compelling, gracious ways, whose every movement was charm, and whose face was that of an angel, not so much for beauty, but for *character*. That was the word that had come to him last night in the cab.

"I believe you," he said solemnly, when she raised her head. Even her hair was just right. "You've probably found something the rest of us have searched for in vain."

"In vain, because not whole-heartedly, perhaps." She thrust deftly, yet without causing pain.

"Perhaps." Then, "Thank you for your beautiful note of last night."

She flashed him a radiant smile. . . . Did she know the power of a smile like that? Perhaps not, for there was not the slightest evidence that she was conscious of her own attractiveness. She was just simply and wholesomely different.

"I've been wondering what happened to *him*," he continued.

Her face clouded. "That's the one thing that concerns me."

"Your silver lining has a cloud, then?"

She smiled, soberly. "I do wish I could know if he is all right."

"You should hope that the scoundrel fell into the water and was eaten by sharks."

Her smile was faint, while a look of pain crossed her face. She spoke slowly, lowering her voice, while her eyelids drew together in a far-away expression. "He was very pitiable."

The silence that followed was tense, but the conversation continued. When she had finished her breakfast, she excused herself and graciously withdrew.

James watched her until she had disappeared, then he turned once more to the newspaper. He felt, strangely, that a rare spirit had departed and that in the departure he had been robbed of something sweet and good, yet something which was not his own. He was surprised that he felt as he did toward her. No other woman had ever moved him like this. There was not the slightest thought of romance in his mind, only a quiet, restful something that made him long, not for her, but for that which made her seem so at peace.

Slowly he scanned the paper, turning aimlessly from page to page. It would soon be ten o'clock when he must arrive at the store.

Grant returned. "Different, isn't she?" he questioned, as he came up.

"Who is she?" James asked in reply.

"I thought you knew her."

"I met her last night — unique personality."

"Entirely different. I supposed you noticed what she did before she ate."

"I'm still under the spell of it."

"Of *her,* you mean."

"Any way you care to put it," James returned, evasively, and rose to his feet. "It's time to relieve Glover at the store. See you at noon, Grant."

"Short ribs, the chef says — so long."

Fownley wanted to stop at the desk to find out where June Darle had come from, but he thought better of it and hastened out, not knowing that he was to face a new crisis before noon.

Ten minutes later he entered his shop. In the window all the latest popular novels were displayed in attractive jackets of every color. "Good morning, Glover," he greeted. "How's business?"

Glover, red-haired and freckled and with a breezy atmosphere about him, answered, "Fine, fine, fine, Mr. Fownley, I've sold ten copies of *Mad World*. That book seems to be taking the country by storm. We'll have to lay in a new supply. Yes, sir."

"That's splendid, Glover. Well, you may run along now until 12:30."

Fownley went to his desk to open his mail and to set himself to answer any that might require immediate attention. But just then someone entered, and he rose quickly, assumed a business air and approached the front of the store. The prospect was a man, well groomed, well tailored.

"I'm looking for a copy of *Mad World*," the stranger announced in a business-like tone. "The library doesn't seem to have it. Someone said I might find it here." He looked about, taking in the store at a glance.

"We've only a few copies left," Fownley said. "They're going fast. I'm ordering fifty more today." He presented the book, a neatly bound volume in an attractive green and white jacket.

"I suppose you've read the book?" the man said to James.

James hadn't. "No, sir, I've been busy, very busy, but I expect to glance through it today. I stocked it because of the demand."

The stranger looked at him appraisingly. "A rather startling book, according to the reviews. At any rate it has some statistics I want. How much is it?"

"One twenty-five."

The man counted out one dollar and twenty-five cents and handed it over. "I should like to introduce myself," he said. "I'm a minister. . . . Warburne's my name." He held out his hand. "Glad to meet you, Mr. ———"

"Fownley . . . Same to you."

Yet Fownley was not sure he was glad to meet anyone who had that name. He searched the face of the man before him and thought he saw a trace of likeness to the Warburne he knew.

"I'll call again," the minister said. "By the way, do you go to church anywhere? . . . Come over to Calvary Church Sunday night. I'm going to use some of the statistics of this book in my sermon."

James watched him, a high wall of prejudice standing between them. Yet from courtesy he inquired, "What is your theme?"

The minister was pleased with the show of interest. "A rather peculiar theme, but a neglected one, I am sure. I shall speak on 'Suicide, the Great American Curse, Its Causes and Its Cure.'"

James started, but regained his composure. Already last night seemed to him like a bad dream.

"There was a suicide in the city last night," the Rev. Mr. Warburne said. "I'm going to get some detailed information about it today if possible, although it seems to be shrouded in mystery."

James was standing on the opposite side of the table. The memory of his experience of last night was like the memory of a nightmare. It still didn't seem true that he was awake. He had been so completely under the spell of the mad desire to kill himself that being in the body seemed scarcely believable. He said nothing, merely looking at the man before him.

"They're not quite sure the case last night was a suicide," the minister went on. "He was drowned in the bay and there was a deep gash on the left jaw which could have been made by a blow of some kind. Well, I must be going. Good day, Mr. Fownley." He opened the door and hurried out.

Fownley stared after him. And as he stood there amidst the silence of the books and the tall shelves, his left hand moved slowly over to his right, his fingers touched, tremblingly, the big diamond set in his ring, while the words of the man who had called himself Warburne pounded dully in his soul: "A gash on his left jaw, which could have been made by a blow of some kind . . . They are not sure it was a suicide . . . *He was drowned in the bay!*"

CHAPTER IV

At fifteen minutes to eight o'clock the following Sunday night, Fownley, in company with Grant Weston, entered the massive stone Calvary Church. Already the lower floor of the huge auditorium was filled, and the incoming throngs were overflowing into the galleries. The two men followed the flow of the crowd, and soon found themselves seated, comfortably, with a good view of the platform.

A friendly buzz of subdued conversation could be heard everywhere — not a note of irreverence, but of friend greeting friend. In a moment the organ began to play and a hush swept over the audience.

"Quite an air of expectancy here tonight," James whispered to his companion.

"I'm curious, myself," was Grant's reply. "It's a cinch someone should speak on the subject Warburne's chosen. Let's hope he doesn't dodge the real issue. I'm in the mood for an old-fashioned, orthodox sermon tonight."

Fownley kept his eyes fixed on the platform, not knowing just what type of sermon his frame of mind called for. It had been a struggle to come at all. Had it not been for the minister's second call at the store he should not have been here.

In due time the opening part of the service was over and the minister rose to speak. Fownley was impressed with his appearance: tall, well-clad, dignified but not solemn, and noticeably composed. "My friends," he began. The voice was clear and challenging and the words carefully enunciated. "I speak tonight on the 'Great American Curse — Suicide,' and upon a greater curse, its causes. I shall hope, in the course of my message, to present the only remedy."

Toward the close of the address James was startled by a terse statement which seemed to exactly fit his own case: *"It is a dimmed or a distorted view of the life after death which permits*

23

this awful epidemic of suicide. If men believed right, they would die right! For they would live as they believed!

"Here is a young man. Old truths which taught a Hell for the lost and a Heaven for the saved, have been renounced. Death ends all, he thinks. A love affair disappoints him. He is crushed and the verdict is self destruction!"

There was more along this line, thrilling, stirring, and convincing. Plainly, the great audience was moved.

At the close of the service an invitation was given for any who wished to accept Jesus Christ as a personal Saviour to let it be known by publicly confessing Him. A number made the Great Decision.

A half hour later the two men paused at the door of James' room. "Come in for a while, Grant, I want to talk with you." Grant had been anticipating this very thing. Something strange in Fownley's attitude, especially noticeable during the past several days, had caused him to wonder if anything were wrong. James' wanting to go to church had strengthened that suspicion. He could sense the tenseness in Fownley's movements; and the soberness of his face was almost startling.

The room itself was restful to the eye and was furnished in thoroughly modern style. Under the floor lamp was a large green and rust mohair chair. Beside it a floor lamp cast a soft glow over everything. The rug, which covered the entire floor, was of oriental design, its colors blending in harmony with everything else in the room.

Fownley opened the conversation, calmly. "Grant, you're in for the role of a father confessor, tonight. I've some things to get off my mind. If I don't, something's going to explode."

"All right, let's hear the worst." Grant said the words somewhat lightly. But James knew there was depth of comradeship behind them. He completed the removal of his shoes and sheathed his feet in brown leather bedroom slippers. Then leaning back in his chair, he said:

"First, I want to know what you think of Warburne's sermon."

Weston looked disappointed. He preferred to hear the confession at once. "I enjoy listening to it — that kind of theology, but I don't believe in it. Haven't for years. All the old foundations have rotted out long ago as far as I am concerned. I liked the sermon, appreciated the fervor and sincerity of the man and I agree with him as to the fact of the suicide crisis, but I can't see his theology."

"But his conclusions — as to the cause, are they not well taken, whether we believe it or not?"

"You mean, that faith in what the Bible teaches concerning the hereafter is the best antidote?"

"Yes."

"Well," — Grant felt for a cigarette. "Smoke, James? You do, don't you?"

James shook his head. "Well, *what?*"

"He's right, I suppose. When a man is driven and tossed by an angry sea, about the only thing that will hold him is a good strong anchor."

James shot another question at his friend: "Listen, Grant, do you believe in Hell, that a man must go to either one place or the other when he — when he bumps himself off?"

"What difference does it make to you, Fownley? What has this to do with the confession?"

"A lot. I've been free from any qualms of conscience for a long time. I don't expect ever to have to shovel coal for fallen Lucifer, but when a fellow meets two sane, educated persons in one week who believe without the shadow of a doubt that the 'wicked shall be turned into hell' and that the 'saved' shall go to the other place, it sort of makes him wonder about these things."

"The preacher and who else?"

James was silent. It was as though he could not utter her name except reverently. "June Darle," he said, and the way he said it made Weston look at him soberly for a moment. Then his face lighted with a smile as he looked about for an ash tray, and his eyes twinkled:

"I forgive you, James, gladly. I suspected it. I'd forgive any man for falling in love with her. I'd do it myself if —"

James rose quickly, his face pale. "You can eliminate the light stuff, Weston, for tonight . . . please. Sorry I don't have an ash

tray . . . there's the fireplace! And now if you'll excuse me."
His eyes took on a weary look. "I'll see you in the morning,
Grant. Good night!"

Grant was on his feet instantly. "I'm sorry, old man, I didn't
realize . . . Forgive me, please. I've been a fool, I . . ."

"That's all right, I just wanted to open up a little. A man
gets that way once in awhile, and when he does he wants sympathetic ears."

"Doubly sorry, Fownley. Maybe next time — if you let me
have a 'next time' . . . Is it too late now?"

"For tonight," James answered, as he turned and walked into
the bathroom.

Alone once more, James reflected, wondering what it was
that made him dismiss Grant as he had and what his friend
would think of him for having done it. His thoughts went at
once to the man who had been drowned in the bay and who was
to be buried tomorrow. The papers had said little about it except that the final verdict of the coroner was that it was a suicide. But James wondered if that were true. And as he heard
the footsteps of Grant in the hall, his eyes fell on the big diamond on his right hand. "Tomorrow," he said, "I must see
June Darle. She may know."

Grant had been gone but a few minutes when James suddenly
halted in his preparations for retiring. Stepping to the bathroom
mirror he examined his face closely. He was still smooth-shaven;
and a few strokes of his comb would fix his hair. He selected a
fresh tie to match the blue of his suit. Five minutes later he
appeared at the desk in the hotel lobby.

"Good evening, Giles," he said to that young man. Giles was
deeply engrossed in a book. He looked up. "Going out, Mr.
Fownley?"

Fownley ignored the question. "Let me see the register."

"She's still here," Giles yawned. "Have you read this new
book? It's all the rage. I suppose you sell it and know all about
it."

James' eyes fell on the green and white jacket of the book
Giles held in his hand. "Yes, I sell it — sell dozens of them

every day. Haven't read it myself yet, but I intend to get into it tomorrow. . . . Listen, Giles, has June Darle checked out yet?" Giles slowly rose to tower a good six inches over Fownley's five foot eleven. "I thought her name was Marlyn."

Again James ignored Giles. One had to do that with him; and Giles in the long run would never notice that he was being rebuked. Everything with him was a part of life and nothing was worth making an extra movement or taking an extra thought to understand. He handed over the register and returned to his reading.

Quickly James ran his eye down the pages till he found what he sought. June Darle was still here. The number of her room was 426. The room directly above his own, he thought, as he pushed the register across the desk. "Call me at eight in the morning," he said, and stepped to the elevator.

As he entered the elevator, he announced, "Fourth floor, please."

The elevator boy had been reading. He inserted a book mark, laid the book aside, and closed the doors of the elevator. "A very interesting book — this, *Mad World,*" he remarked to James. "Kinda awful, though, in some places. Just think! Every twenty-nine minutes somebody in the world commits suicide."

"Don't care to think of it!" James returned, somewhat abruptly. It was enough that he had tried to do the deed himself and had failed.

At the fourth floor he stepped out and the doors clicked shut behind him. He waited till the light on the wall board showed that the elevator had reached the first floor. Then he turned toward room 426. A peculiar emotion gripped him and he began to have serious misgivings as to that which he was about to do. Should he ask her to accompany him to the first floor lobby where they might be assured of seclusion at this hour of the night? And where — he found himself thinking — he might watch the glow of her eyes as she talked of "satisfaction?" Or should he immediately broach the question concerning the man who had drowned, find out at once if she knew whether he were the one who had annoyed her on the pier that night, and then, thanking her, return to his own room?

There was a light shining through the transom above her door. Well, here he was. He must not stand here undecided. Fownley was seldom undecided in anything. He would knock at the door at once. The proper way would have been to send up a note asking for an interview. But who cared for things proper when things pressing were demanding immediate action?

He knocked, three clear raps — not too loudly, except for the last one, when the set in his ring struck the door sharply. A quick vision of the events of the Friday before came back to sicken him.

There was a rustling within. Then footsteps approached the door.

James was unprepared for what his eyes saw. He had, without thinking, pictured June coming graciously to the door to welcome him. She would be dressed in a simple, black, long-sleeved frock. Her light brown hair would be perfectly dressed and she would be smiling. Twice since that morning at the breakfast table, he had seen her, each time with greater pleasure. She would look the same tonight, perhaps.

The last time he had seen her was Saturday afternoon when he had sought to speak with her about the Bay suicide; but she had steered the conversation to other things, as if she had wanted to forget.

It seemed an eternity before the door opened, during which time a startling thought presented itself. If it should be publicly known that he had struck the man, had, perhaps, been responsible for his drowning he, James Fownley, would not be the only one involved. *June Darle would be implicated also!* And, suddenly, he could not bear to think what the consequences might be to her. . . . No, he must not even ask her about this thing.

There had been so little of it in the papers that perhaps she had not even heard. He suddenly wished that he had not come and he chided himself that he had been thinking too much of his own interests — of his own heavy conscience. Why should he throw upon a girl a burden which might — if it could— cause to fade the smile of contentment which shone upon her face?

But now the door was opening.

"*Marlyn!*" he gasped.

CHAPTER V

If Marlyn had been gorgeous that Friday night when she had suddenly appeared in Fownley's room, she was even more so tonight. James was speechless, stunned by her beauty. She was resplendent in a long, wine leaf velvet dress. James' senses reeled in a vain effort to retain his composure. He could think of nothing for the moment but her ravishing beauty, while he visualized himself swinging to slow music with Marlyn in his arms. Marlyn always made him think of "soft lights and sweet music."

He stirred himself. He must not stand gaping like an enamored fool. He must say something. What was she doing in Miss Darle's room? He started to speak, but her words came first: -

"Come in, Jimmy. I'm all alone — for a while. Miss Darle will be back in twenty minutes. You wanted to see her, I suppose."

"I want to talk with her . . . alone . . . if that will be satis- factory with you." There was a touch of bitterness in his voice.

Marlyn stepped back to allow him to enter, her very movement an invitation to him to cross the threshold. But James did not move. He did not trust himself to be alone with her for even twenty minutes. He feared lest he be caught up and swirled as in other days, into the very vortex of her charms, lest he relent of his decision to have nothing more to do with her.

But she was politely insistent. "You need not be afraid. I have almost changed my mind about you since becoming acquainted with Miss Darle — she's mad about you —"

"Listen, Marlyn!" James' voice was cold and his face a livid white. "I've come to see Miss Darle. Does she or does she not have this room? And if she does, when will she be back?"

"If you care to see her you may come in and wait. I am her secretary during her stay in the city, and just now you may make your appointments through me. If you don't believe me, then — good night!"

She started to close the door, but he sprang suddenly to action and entered the room. "We're leaving the door open," he said, grimly, "till Miss Darle comes."

The atmosphere was strained as he seated himself to wait for the woman he now decided he really wanted to see, if not to speak to her about that which had impelled him here, then to let Marlyn Favis know of a certainty that he had not come to see her.

Marlyn, lounging lazily on a divan, sighed restively. "You're not even civil to me, James," she pouted. "You act as though I were some dangerous reptile, or else a politician, trying to inveigle you into voting for him."

"Well?"

"I don't like it. I want you to be nice to me. But I suppose that since I'm only her secretary, my chances are *nil*. Oh well, I can wait."

"That will be fine," James thrust with sarcasm. "And I'll help you."

She flashed him a pained look while her lips formed again an ill-humored pout.

James could guess that she was hurt over having lost him, but he knew that it was her wounded pride more than her disappointed love which hurt. And in that he found some satisfaction. What was this new role she was playing now? Secretary to Miss Darle? How had they become acquainted? What did Miss Darle do? Why did she need a secretary? She certainly was not, like Marlyn, out to make her fortune. She was probably trying to help Marlyn. Curious companionship: a woman of refinement, education, beauty of soul, faith; and Marlyn! True; there was in Marlyn, education, wit, beauty — physical beauty — but there was no faith! And he sometimes thought — no soul!

He glanced at his watch. Ten minutes had elapsed, and he could wait another eternity for the other ten to pass. Rack his brain as he would he could think of nothing to say to Miss Darle when she would arrive. Since he had made up his mind not to mention the Bay suicide, there was nothing that he might say to explain why he had called at this hour of the night. Oh well, what matter? He could wait till she came and then say the first thing that came to his mind. He could trust himself that much anyway.

He smothered a yawn, at the same time smothering his desire to yawn perceptibly, that it might appear to Marlyn that he was bored by her presence.

Suddenly she rose, crossed to the writing desk and returned with a book. "Have you seen this?" she questioned. He reached out his hand to receive the green- and white-jacketed book. "This is the third time in the last half hour! Thanks, yes, we sell it."

"I think it's perfectly horrid. It gives me the shudders. I couldn't sleep last night — ugh. Why should anyone want to write such terrible things?"

He smiled inwardly, glad that anything could impress Marlyn so deeply. He *must* read the book. Perhaps he could open it right now . . . for a few moments.

There was a rap at the door. "Is Miss June Darle here?" a voice asked. "Telegram for June Darle."

Marlyn had answered the knock. "Miss Darle will be here any moment," she said. "I will hold the message for her."

The boy bowed and disappeared, while Marlyn returned to stand before Fownley's chair. "That's the second wire today. Quite a popular person, this Miss Darle. And you should see her mail. It all comes from Denver. I suppose she has many friends there, although one would scarcely expect them all to write every day. She gets a dozen or more letters in each mail."

James looked up at her. "She told you to tell me this?"

Marlyn bit her lip. "I'd tell you anything, James."

He felt the spell of her personality and he set himself to fight it. "I think I'll read *Mad World,*" he said with a gesture as if to dismiss her.

The phone rang and she turned to answer it. "Calling Miss Marlyn Favis," a voice said. Marlyn waited for the message. James heard her say, "Yes . . . yes . . . I'm here . . . not tonight? — What? Wait, there's a telegram . . . hello! . . . hello! She's gone!" Marlyn said, as she turned about, "and she's not coming back until morning. 'Unavoidably delayed,' she said."

James remembered the other night when June might have been permanently. "delayed." He was on his feet. "Where was she calling from? Did she say?" he asked, authoritatively, his fears seizing him. "Tell me!" he demanded, "where did she call from?"

Marlyn wilted. "I — I don't know!" she said. "She said something about the Knickerbocker, but I couldn't get it."

James' eyes blazed. "I don't believe you," he said. "Tell me — no! never mind — I'll find her. I'll take her telegram to her. At least, I needn't wait here. If you want someone to talk to, call up Warburne from the dead, and talk to him." Taking the yellow envelope he left the room.

In his own room he stopped only long enough to get his hat and coat and to trace the call. In the street he hailed a cab and directed: "Oakland, the Knickerbocker Hotel."

In the room he had left behind, Marlyn crossed to the mirror and surveyed herself. "Don't worry, Miss Marlyn, he'll be 'Jimmy' yet, and kissing your hand for smiles." She turned this way and that, every movement one of practised grace.

Again there was a knock at the door. "James again," she thought, "I knew he'd be back. This time I'll —"

But it was not James. Marlyn gasped and things went black before her eyes. The man at the door was — *Warburne!*

"I — you — where — what?" she began. But he laughed and something in the laugh sounded like reality and she regained her presence of mind.

He did not wait for her to invite him in, but entered quickly and closed the door. A second later he had her in his arms. "I've come back to you, Marlyn . . . You — you're lovely tonight. Same old Marlyn, aren't you? Always irresistible!" His words were quick, yet easily uttered.

Then she spoke. "It isn't you — it can't be. You were drowned." She caught at the lapels of his coat, and standing away from him, looked into his eyes.

"False report — false on purpose, for one of those neat little schemes of mine that nobody needs to know anything about. It was to my advantage to be thought dead. But I decided to come back to life."

She drew him to the divan. But he refused to be seated. "Business first, Marlyn. Are you still mine or not?"

She hesitated. She could conceal the truth within a half truth. "I am no one else's, Graig." And with the words she sent her smile.

His eyes rested upon her, as if in doubt as to the integrity of what she had said. "Why are you here? It took me an hour to find you. And now you are in a room that belongs to somebody else, an angel-child."

Marlyn lifted her eyebrows. "You know her?"

"I've got a psalm-singing uncle who introduced me to her. She's good-looking, but she's too good for me."

"Let's have the business, Graig."

He returned to the former question. "Why are you in Miss Darle's room?"

She laughed. "I met her in the lounge the other day, and worked on her. She's going to try to convert me, Graig; and she's going to pay me meanwhile. I am her companion while she is in the city. I show her places of interest, the museums, the historical parks, libraries, and hospitals, and help her with her mail. She's a charming girl and altogether good: doesn't smoke, drink, dance or say things. She's an angel."

"I know these angels," he grunted, almost discourteously. "But where is she now?"

Marlyn smiled to herself, yet fully aware that he would notice it, and wanting him to. "She's in Oakland at the Knickerbocker. Mr. Fownley is there, too."

Warburne started. "Fownley!"

"Mr. James Fownley. He left this room less than twenty minutes ago."

"This room!" Graig's look was one of bewildered surprise.

"This very room. We had a lovely visit. He's gone to protect Miss Darle, because he was afraid she was in danger. The fool! He'll have his trip for nothing! I didn't tell him she said she was staying with a friend of hers, Miss Silvers."

Warburne's face changed. "Silvers?" he barked. "Did she say any first name?"

Marlyn turned in astonishment. "Why, no. Why?"

"This is just something else that you'd better not know about." He turned, fiercely, to the door. "I'll be back — tonight!" he said. He seized his hat, and went hurriedly down the hall.

CHAPTER VI

Things had been happening at the Knickerbocker Hotel.

June Darle had asked Marlyn if she would like to accompany her to church, as she wanted to hear Dr. Warburne's address. But Marlyn had refused, saying:

"To church? I should say not. The gay life for me. But you go, you'd be an adornment to any church. If I had a face like yours, I'd pray for wings to match. No, if you really don't mind, I'll stay here until you come back."

June appraised her. "You are a beautiful creature, Miss Favis, and you need only one thing more to make your beauty genuine." She paused. "I am being frank with you, too frank, perhaps, but since you won't hear Dr. Warburne's sermon, I shall preach you one, myself — you need more *soul beauty!*"

And Marlyn had had that to think over as she sat under the floor lamp and read. It had been the peculiar agreement of the book she was reading with what Miss Darle had said that had angered her. Last night she had sat up till past midnight, reading, fascinated but rebelling at every paragraph, as she found her character being ruthlessly analyzed. Yet, today she had eagerly awaited an opportunity to read further.

At Calvary Church June listened intently to the message. From time to time, however, her attention was drawn to the peculiar actions of a young woman who was seated in the pew in front of her and somewhat to the right.

Whenever the minister came to some climax in his address and drove home his point, the girl's face would turn pale and she would clasp her hands tightly and bite her lips as if in agony. And once when the speaker thundered, authoritatively: "*Death does not end all!*" a look of horror crossed her face.

The girl was dressed simply, in brown. The frayed sleeves of her coat were darned carefully until they were scarcely noticeable. "Poor thing," June murmured to herself, "she needs

34

a friend." And suddenly she resolved to find out more about her. Where had she seen that face before? Or had she?

When the service came to a close the girl rose and hurried with the crowd to the exit. June followed her with difficulty, awaiting her first opportunity to speak to her. She felt that some fierce struggle was going on in the girl's mind; and she knew that she must continue to follow her and help — if she could.

In the street the girl hailed a cab, and June arrived just in time to hear her direct the driver to the Knickerbocker Hotel in Oakland. "And hurry!" she heard her say.

June was accustomed to emergencies. Her life had been one of many and varied experiences. She *must* follow the girl with the anguished face. Some mighty drama of life was about to be enacted and she must be there to witness it, to have some part in it, and, perhaps, to change things.

A few moments later she said to her own cab driver, "Take me to the Knickerbocker Hotel in Oakland! If you ever drove fast, do it now. It's a matter of life and death!"

He saw her determined look and accepted the five dollar bill which she pressed into his hand. "Thank ye, Miss, I'll smash the records. Hold on tight." A moment later he was making good his boast.

It was as if they had raced neck and neck with the other cab and had lost. June spoke, hurriedly, to the man at the desk; "Can you let me have a pass key?" she said in a low tone as she presented her card.

The man evidently was familiar with the name on the card. He immediately pressed a key into her hand.

"If I need help," she whispered, "I'll call you."

He watched her as she took the next elevator up.

At the seventh floor June stepped out and at room 792 paused for breath, the key in her hand. 792, was the room the girl had taken. She knew she must not wait even for a moment. Situations like this had occurred before. Her intuition was backed by experience and wisdom. She listened, briefly. She knew that the Knickerbocker was an up-to-the-minute hotel and that it was impossible for the door to be locked in such a way but that she could immediately gain entrance with the key. The sounds from within told her that something was happening. Immediately she knocked.

The movements inside ceased, then began once more. June heard the window open. Quickly she applied the key and thrust open the door. She was not one moment too soon. The girl was before the open window, ready to jump. In a flash June rushed across the room and seized her just in time to keep her from leaping to the street below.

"Stop!" the girl cried, "let me alone! I want to die!"

"Oh, no, you don't, you mustn't!" June struggled fiercely, until she managed to drag the hysterical girl from the window and to close it. She closed the door also.

For a moment the girl stared at her, wildly. "Who — who are you?" Then she began to sob, and she buried her face against her rescuer's shoulder. "Oh, why didn't you let me do it?" she cried. "I — I don't want to live. I fought all day to get courage enough, and now —"

Her voice went high again and she began to cry once more. June's arms enfolded her tenderly, while she kissed her and sought to dry her tears. "You are a brave girl," her voice said, soothingly, as she stroked the disheveled curls. Golden curls they were — artificially golden — but beautiful nevertheless. "Things are going to be different from now on."

The girl suddenly roused herself, and as if in a daze looked at Miss Darle. "Different? Oh no, not in a world like this. Only in another! I can't stand *this* world!"

June smiled. "Neither can I. I haven't been standing it for some time. I've been *in* it but not *of* it."

Still the girl stared. "Who — who are you?" she exclaimed wildly. "You don't sound human! Have I —?" A bitter smile formed on her lips to die instantly. "Have I really found another world after all?"

June laughed, softly. "No, not yet, my dear, but you shall soon. I'm going to tell you about a world within a world. But come, tell me who *you* are, and why you were in such a hurry to get to the first floor!" She felt that a lighter mood might help just now.

But the girl's face was still sober, as with anguished expression she pointed to the writing desk. "That note will tell you. I carried it all day."

June saw that she really wanted her to read the note. She reached for it. It was in a sealed envelope. Before opening it she said: "I saw you in church tonight. Didn't Dr. Warburne's sermon convince you?"

The girl cringed. "Dr. *who?* What was that name?"

"Dr. Warburne."

The girl's face went white. "I — oh — yes, his sermon was good, but I couldn't believe all that. I didn't want to hear that kind of sermon. I wanted to hear something else — something to make me doubt the Bible . . . So I could get more courage to — to — find a way out. I got in the wrong church. I should have been more careful."

"The right church, my dear, and a real church. Those other places aren't *churches*. Not at all."

She opened the envelope. It said on the outside, "To My Mother."

The girl watched as she read. When June finished, she asked, "Well, can you blame me?"

June fixed her eyes upon her. "What is your last name, Mary? You've signed your first only."

"My last name doesn't count," she answered, bitterly. "It's Silvers."

"So you wanted to be a movie star?"

The anguished face of the girl relaxed a little. Whoever this woman was who had befriended her, she was, at least, kind. Somehow she felt free to talk. "Yes, we all did, but we didn't have the 'brains,' they told us. Beauty without brains is no good in Hollywood — except for 'extras,' and extras can starve for all the management cares. If your beauty fades and you have nothing but 'brains' left, then you're out anyway."

"Poor Mary! How long is it since you've been home?"

"Home! That word cuts like a knife. Four years at least."

June was still stroking the curls and studying the face of the girl. They were seated now on the divan. Mary's face, in spite of its make-up, was one of beauty; the features revealed character.

"Oh," the girl continued desperately, "no one cared — no one was interested — in the rest of us. We bought our own clothes and paid for them . . ." She bit her lip, desperately.

"You didn't make the grade?"

"I didn't — thousands of us don't."

"How have you lived?"

"I haven't — I've walked the streets, scrubbed floors — and —*starved!* Oh, it's terrible." She went into sobs again. "I don't want to live."

"But," June began, "surely there was some way."

Mary sat up suddenly. "There *was* a way, but I couldn't — I *wouldn't* — I'd die first."

Her eyes took on a wild expression and she shuddered. "It's awful — *terrible!* Oh, I've seen them — ex-stars, some of them, driving up and down the boulevards in Cadillac cars, with only a gallon of gasoline; seen them stop at restaurants and tea rooms."

Her voice went high again and she talked hysterically:

"Seen them sit at tables with strange men, and seen the men in the end pay for the meal. I've seen them — girls from the small towns like myself, fight on until the last penny was gone, not daring to tell the folks back home. Seen them take waitress jobs, dime store clerking — Oh, I've seen them come home at night tired and ready to drop from walking all day. Seen them give up at last to take anything: dance hall jobs, scrubbing floors — even to walking the streets. Oh, God pity them! There are thousands of them."

Suddenly she stopped, exhausted, and leaned back against June's friendly shoulder. "I took the best way — I — but you stopped me. Why did you stop me?"

June suddenly looked at her wrist watch. She must call her hotel. "Excuse me for just a moment," she said. She crossed hastily to the telephone. To the man at the desk below she said,

"Everything's all right. Yes, we're staying here . . . both of us . . . for tonight."

Then she called the Walhurst.

A moment later she turned to her new friend. "I'll stay with you tonight, dear. Do you mind? I've a perfectly wonderful plan for you if you'll let me. May I?"

CHAPTER VII

Due to a traffic accident Fownley's cab was delayed. Consequently when he arrived at the Knickerbocker he was only a few moments ahead of Warburne. The man at the desk was at first reluctant to allow him to go to June's room. But when he saw the telegram which was to be James' ostensible reason for coming, he said, "All right," but added, warningly, "She will not want to be disturbed."

Fownley's pulse leaped. In lightning flashes he pictured a multitude of things that might have happened. But to each conjecture the quiet face of the girl said a positive "No."

At room 792 he knocked. The door was answered at once.

"Miss Darle?" he asked, hat in hand, top coat still on.

"Mr. Fownley! Come in."

Fownley obeyed, conscious of a coldness in her demeanor. He could not tell her that he had come to watch over her. "I have brought a telegram," he answered. He could feel her aloofness, now more than ever.

"Thank you," she said, "I was expecting it. Miss Favis just called to tell me you were coming with it. Excuse me." She tore open the yellow envelope and read, hastily.

Replacing the message in the envelope she tossed it carelessly to the writing desk. Then she turned to the girl. "Mary, this is Mr. James Fownley. Miss Mary Silvers."

Fownley bowed, his eyes resting on the face of the girl, who merely nodded and smiled faintly.

June continued, her voice suddenly softening, "I have been deeply disappointed in you, Mr. Fownley." She hesitated. He was stunned. What had happened to change her attitude toward him? What had *he* done? Had he —?

He thought of Marlyn. Marlyn had called about the telegram and Marlyn perhaps had said angry, bitter, false things. He was about to speak but she did not permit him.

40

"There need be no explanation, Mr. Fownley. Had it not been for my timely arrival and for the intervening Providence of God you would have been responsible for murder tonight, for a self-murder. Here — take this and go." She thrust into his hand a small book. "Miss Silvers bought this at your store Saturday."

Before James could realize what was happening he found himself in the hall and the door being closed upon him. He was astounded, bewildered. He glanced at the book in his hand. He recalled that at one time it had been one of his best sellers, that it was still popular. The stamp of his store, "The Green Front Book Shop," was on the inside cover.

His eyes rested on the gold stamped title, *De-throning God.* To him there was nothing particularly astonishing or shocking about that. As he quickly turned the pages he caught the flash of an unusual sentence and he turned back to find it.

"We have proved, then, that there is no God, now to explode the theory of existence after death!" He read on and to his slowly awakening senses there came the realization that this book was a treatise on atheism, written by an atheist for the avowed purpose of producing atheists. On the fly leaf was printed, "Text book, designed for use in our Canadian and American Sunday Schools, Recommended by A. A. A. A." (American Association for the Advancement of Atheism).

James was so absorbed that he was unaware of footsteps approaching. Their sound came nearer and nearer on the soft-carpeted hallway. Instinctively he stepped aside without looking up. He was not in the mood now to see anyone or to have anyone glimpse the scowl on his face.

With a sense of mingled disgust and disappointment he closed the book and directed his steps toward the elevator. Thus he did not see Warburne as he passed. But Warburne had seen *him*.

In room 792 June Darle and Mary Silvers were engaged in animated conversation.

"You don't mean, my dear, that you have ceased to believe at all in God and in His Son, Jesus Christ!"

Mary burst out passionately: "Oh, I don't believe in anything or anybody. Why should I? Men fight each other like cats and dogs, the whole world — if newspapers tell the truth — is on the verge of another war, with every country arming, the big strike in Frisco is still smouldering. There are strikes all over the nation and all over the world. Even in America, which is so rich, women and children are starving, men wander up and down because they are out of work — homeless, penniless, miserable, unloved. Thousands of girls walk the streets to find work. The beer parlors are wide open, filled with lazy, drunken men. Oh, even in high circles, if there is a higher circle, the world is cruel and heartless. There is no love anywhere, nothing but hate, greed and — oh, who could believe in God in a world like this!"

June fixed her eyes on the flushed face of the girl. "Tell me," she requested gently, "has there been some one great sorrow in your life aside from your disappointment concerning a stage career?" She knew that this bitterness often was the outgrowth of some one tragic event in the life of its victim.

The girl bit her lip while her beautiful eyes filled once more with tears. June crossed to her side and embraced her tenderly. "Never mind, dear, you needn't tell me — not now, nor ever — unless you choose. You must rest now."

It was at this moment that Warburne approached the door. In response to his knock June went quietly to the door, rather expecting that Fownley had returned. Wisdom cautioned her to inquire, "Who is there?"

Warburne's voice was smooth and gentle. "An old friend on a matter of importance."

June thought a moment. Then in a flash she turned to Mary and motioned her to hide in the bathroom. "Let him think I am alone," her lips said.

Mary obeyed, her eyes questioning.

June opened the door and Warburne entered, bowing graciously. When the door had been closed, he asked, "Alone? I thought you would be flanked by women police. I am fortunate."

June did not meet his smile. Her face was sober and her body rigid. She stood near the telephone.

"You had better stand," she said as he made as if to sit down.

He scowled and his eyes searched the room. "All alone? No company?" he asked.

"Unfortunately not alone now," she said. "But I hope to be soon." She moved nearer the telephone, her hand on the receiver. "And now, Mr. Warburne, you may go."

"Thank you," he bowed, mockingly. "I intended to inquire after your health, but I see you are perfectly well." He paused at the door as if to speak further, but her eyes forbade him. With a smile, he opened the door and walked down the hall.

CHAPTER VIII

It was ten o'clock Monday morning. June was back in her own room at the Walhurst. Before her on her desk lay the morning mail. There was little today that required immediate attention, so she sat there musing for a moment.

A few moments later she was ready for the street. .

Pausing at Marlyn's room she knocked. Marlyn answered the door, begged her to come in while she dressed. They could have breakfast together.

"Sorry," June said, "but I've a few errands to do now. You'll be ready at two o'clock? Call at my room then."

In the street June directed her steps toward the Green Front Book Shop. There were some things she wanted to discuss with James Fownley.

Immediately after breakfast she had escorted Mary to the home of a very dear friend in a quiet, residential district of the city, where she promised to call for her that night at eight o'clock.

"Good-bye until then, Mary dear," she said, as she pressed her hand, affectionately.

"You've been so good to me," Mary replied, her lip quivering. "I think I see it differently now. You'll be sure to come tonight at eight?"

"Right on the dot — don't forget Psalms 34:7."

"I won't. How could I — ever?"

The awning of the Green Front Book Shop came into view and June braced herself for the task before her. Tremendous issues were at stake, she believed. She must talk "straight" to James Fownley.

True, he had saved her life only a few nights ago and last night he had tried to help her again. She was not unappreciative, nevertheless she knew that she must not allow these services to deter her from what she was convinced was her immediate duty.

She paused at the store window, admiring the clever arrangement of the books within. But her eyes narrowed in disapproval as she read some of the titles and recognized them for the type of books they were — popular, but "diabolic." That was the word that came to her mind and formed itself on her lips.

"Good morning, madam! A beautiful morning! Anything I can do for you? Any book I may show you? We have everything that's new —" It was Glover who thus greeted her.

June smiled at his friendliness, tolerating his profusion of speech. "May I see the proprietor?"

"Sorry, madam, very sorry, but he is not here just now. He'll be in most any moment. He is just a little late today. Will you wait in his office?"

"Thank you, I'll browse about. I see you sell *Mad World.*"

"Yes, ma'am, that's our best seller right now. I've sold ten copies this morning; two to a minister, one to a lawyer, three to a Sunday school teacher and —"

"You sell this book?" she interrupted politely. She touched as if with loathing fingers the covers of a smaller book.

"I — yes, yes, ma'am," Glover stammered, "we sell that too — I — I'm sorry to say." He finished somewhat breathless, yet with a note of conviction in his voice.

She studied his face a moment, deciding that she liked him in spite of his verbosity, discerning his sincerity as he uttered the last statement.

"Yes, ma'am," he explained. "I think it's — oh — sacrilegious — such — shocking things." He seemed to feel that she was agreeing with him.

On the previous night things had been happening to Fownley to prepare him for this morning's interview. Entirely unaware that his avowed enemy had passed him in the hall of the Knickerbocker, he continued on his way to the elevator.

At the desk he paused long enough to allow the man in charge to recognize him and with the book still in his hand he entered the street. The clock on a distant church spire was striking midnight. Across the street was Grandview Park. Feeling a sudden desire to be alone where he could think, he made his way thither. It was a night not unlike the Friday night before except for the wind, which was more quiet. Nor was it quite so cool tonight, although the temperature here seldom went very low. The moon had grown slightly in proportion and consequently in brightness.

"So I might have been responsible for murder!" he mused. The words recalled vividly the events of the other night. What difference, he asked himself, between actually taking the life of another and being merely "responsible"?

He found a lonely bench behind a clump of bushes and sat down, drawing his top coat closer about him. The pain that had been stabbing him so relentlessly since he had learned of the "Bay suicide" had been hard to bear. There had been some consolation in knowing he had saved the girl from drowning and, he reasoned, it was almost worth it when one considered the kind of girl she was. His own rash attempt at suicide he had dismissed from his mind, glad, at least partly, that he had not succeeded. In fact all day he had found himself almost happy, especially in those moments when he was able to forget other things of a more depressing nature.

"I have been disappointed in you tonight." That was the thing that had cut him. And then to be ushered from the room by June Darle! The girl who prayed — whose face read, "Peace!"

He held the book in his hand, the gold stamped title plainly visible in the moonlight. He gazed at it with mingled emotion. *De-throning God.*

"She bought it at your store yesterday!" He shrugged. She needn't be so quick at drawing conclusions. What if the girl *had* tried to commit suicide after reading the book! Was that his fault? The business of a book shop was to give the people what they wanted, wasn't it? It most certainly was, he told himself. With his jaw set, and his mind fully made up to tell June Darle what he thought of her hasty judgment he rose to his feet.

"Just a minute there, mister! Stick 'em right straight up."

Fownley turned to face the muzzle of a pistol held in a steady, gloved hand. A handkerchief was tied over the lower part of the face of his assailant.

"Keep your trap shut and shove them mitts up — quick!" the voice barked, while the muzzle of the gun pressed against Fownley's ribs.

Fownley obeyed, sullenly reluctant. It took only a few minutes for the man to relieve him of his watch, his diamond ring and his pocketbook.

"Thank you, mister, you're real accommodatin'. Here's a dime for street car fare in case you have a long ways to go. Now don't get talkative with the cops for twenty minutes, see? Someone might be watchin' you."

The thug started to back away, then suddenly he stooped, picked up the book Fownley had dropped.

A low whistle escaped his lips and he laughed, a harsh, gutteral laugh which made him cough. "Ha! Ha! A religious guy, eh? *Re-throning God!* Well, let me tell you, mister, that's a bigger job than you might think. Well — so long, thanks a lot." He tossed the book with a disdainful gesture at James' feet and hurried away.

Fownley, in spite of his anger at the insolence of the thief, was inwardly amused at the words "religious guy." Nothing could be farther from the truth, he told himself. He picked up the book. The letter "D" *could* have been taken for an "R" — here in the moonlight at least.

With only a dime in his pocket and with street cars running only now and then at this hour of the night he resolved at first to walk home, then thought better of it and hurried back to the Knickerbocker. There he explained what had happened, cashed a check, and a half hour later was in his room at the Walhurst. He smiled grimly as his eyes rested for a moment on the green swastika pattern of the Persian rug on the floor, the green typifying "devotion" and the swastika "good luck."

He could stand the loss of his watch and the money, but the diamond ring was a treasure he did not care to lose. To report to the police had been his first impulse, but then, he reasoned, perhaps it would be just as well if the ring were "lost," at least until long after the "Bay suicide" was forgotten. And so thinking, he tried to sleep.

In the morning he was considerably refreshed and he entered the dining room smiling.

Grant brought him a glass of water. "Forgiven me yet, Fownley?" he questioned, as he readjusted the silverware to suit his fancy. Fownley accepted the proffered menu card and placed his order. "I've forgotten all about it," he said in reply, and his tone confirmed the words.

Grant was off with the order. A few moments later he came back to James' table. Curiosity was written on his face. He simply must find out a few things, yet he was wise enough to know that this was not the time. He had noticed, of course, that June Darle had not come down to breakfast.

A few moments later Grant paused by the table and remarked, casually: "Beautiful day today! Good day for the fight."

"Fight?" Fownley was disinterested.

"The political fight."

"Oh! not concerned, Grant. If we get a change of Governors it's O.K. with me and if we don't that's O.K., too."

"You don't care then if we turn Socialistic?"

"Don't care if we turn completely Russian."

"Well, you'd better keep tuned in on EPIC if I know anything," was Grant's final remark, as Fowney left the dining room.

On the way to his store he resolved determinedly that he would lay aside completely the disturbing thoughts of the past few days; and, when he had, at first opportunity, expressed his opinion on a few things to June Darle, he would proceed insofar as possible, to take life as it came, drinking deeply at its sparkling fountains of pleasure. Perhaps he might yet go back to Marlyn. She could afford him some enjoyment at least. The morning paper had set his mind at rest in regard to the "Bay suicide." One statement had sufficed. It said, "The man was short and stocky, and wore a heavy overcoat." The description was the very opposite of the man who had fallen under Fownley's blow.

And so meditating, he arrived at the Green Front Book Shop.

When he had received his caller and learned that she wished to speak with him alone, he led her into his office, seated her in an easy chair and with the door closed, he was ready for the interview to begin.

But when he read the serene beauty of her face he wavered somewhat in his decision of last night to express his opinion of her judgment. He waited calmly for her to begin the conversation.

"Mr. Fownley." Her voice was low and controlled; he was instantly conscious of the power of her personality.

"I hope that you will not decide that I am ungrateful for what you have done for me. I realize that you saved my life last Friday night and I appreciate deeply your thought of me last night and your kindness in bringing the telegram. But what I have to say this morning I am sure will not be altogether agreeable—it will not be pleasurable to you nor will it be easy for me to tell you.

"In the first place, let me say frankly and unashamedly that I am a Christian, a believer in the Lord Jesus Christ, and am, I trust, a sincere follower of Him. My philosophy of life is based on the Bible, the Word of God, and I accept it gladly as my rule of faith and practice. Since coming to know Him as my personal Saviour and Friend, all my views on worldly things, in fact on nearly everything in life, have been changed. Old-fashioned? Yes. But as fresh and satisfying as the old-fashioned sunshine and the glorious hills and mountains."

She paused, aware of his respectful attention but inwardly pained as she read his expression of tolerant skepticism.

Her purse lay in her lap and in her hand she held tightly a copy of *De-throning God*. A bitter smile crossed her face as she hastened to say, "Please do not understand me to have said all this in apology for what may be considered peculiar views. They are not an apology but an explanation. They are the foundation of that which I wish to tell you, not a mere sedative to lessen the pain of the operation."

He smiled at that and resolved that he was going to enjoy this interview in spite of its unpleasant aspects. He could tolerate the religious embellishments, he was sure. So he set himself to listen. But his anticipation of enjoyment was cut short a moment later when the "operation" actually began. He was also unprepared for the abrupt termination of the interview.

"A mere white-washing of the bare, ugly facts will not do, Mr. Fownley. The crisis of the age is upon us. Everywhere there is evidence of a revival among God's people and thousands are being swept into the Church of Christ. This of course has drawn the fire of the enemy in a more fierce onset than ever. Also, it has served and is serving its ultimate purpose — preparing the true Christians for the rapture at the coming again of Christ.

"But you must admit that America — in fact, the whole world — seems to be headed for terrible chaos." She paused, waiting for his assent to what she had said.

"What's the difference?" he asked, shrugging his shoulders. "There isn't any God anyway." He had heard one sermon last night and had had difficulty enough in erasing its impressions. Was he to listen to another this morning?

"What difference!" She looked at him, astonished. Then suddenly reading his thoughts and his unbelief, she rose to her feet, her eyes blazing. "Mr. Fownley, when I said what I did last night about being disappointed in you I said exactly what I felt. I was and I am — deeply so. Your kind and gentle behavior had led me to respect you, to think highly of you as a man and, if not a Christian, then one who might at least be sympathetic. But —"

Her eyes narrowed with intensity while she looked upon him. "I think I understand now how you can sell such a book as this. You have no faith in God, you live for self and the cheap pleasures this world has to offer. You have certain standards of right and wrong, beautiful in themselves, but borrowed, not inherent. If the 'Four A's' wants to spread its satanic propaganda to undermine our churches, homes and schools, to rot the moral fibre of our country, to rob men of faith in God, to make suicide and murder and all manner of crime and sin plausible, it is welcome to use your store as a medium! And *you* as its agent! You sell good books — yes; but you sell also trash and filth. I repeat what I said last night: If Mary Silvers had committed suicide you would have been at least partly responsible. You sold her the book without warning her that it was poison: and the book was the Devil's tool to dim her eyes to the horrors of a Christless eternity!

"Good day, Mr. Fownley, and may God save you in the only way He can save anyone—through His Son. Some day I hope to claim you for a brother — in — *Him!*"

Her eyes softened and little pools of tears formed there. Abruptly she turned. She did not wait for him, but opened the door herself and stepped outside.

Silently, hurriedly she swept down the length of the store to the outer door, dropped a dollar bill in Glover's hand in payment for the book she carried and was gone.

Alone in his office James reflected on the interview which had had such an unexpected and, to him, unsatisfying termination.

"A 'Doctor Jekyll and Mr. Hyde,'" he said aloud as he recalled the sudden change in her demeanor. And yet, he admitted to himself, the 'Mr. Hyde' manifestation had betrayed no evidence of ill temper, nor had there been any display whatsoever of a lack of self-control. Not once during her upbraiding of him had her face lost its look of peace, in spite of the fact that she had disturbed his own calm to no little degree.

He returned to his desk and sat down. "The little preacheress!" he muttered. He felt chastised. He was chagrined that he had not taken the situation in hand and expressed his own opinion on a few things.

These women! Either extremely worldly or extremely "religious," one almost as bad as the other.

As he continued to seek to alleviate the pain by thinking of what might have been and what later on should be there came stealing into his consciousness another impression, at first startling and then altogether pleasant. How he had arrived at this conviction, which as yet was only a half conviction, he did not know. Nevertheless it was there, knocking firmly at the door of his mind and persistently seeking admittance and approval: *June Darle was the most unusual woman he had ever known; he must forget his wounded pride and become better acquainted with her.*

June in her room was thinking her own thoughts. It was still thirty minutes before lunch time. She sat at her desk deliberating soberly on the things that had happened at the Green Front Book Shop. When she had left her room this morning it had been with a different plan in view. In her prayer for guidance, just before leaving, she had said:

"O Father, Thou hast sent him into my life and through him hast spared me to continue in the work to which I am called. And oh, I am so thankful. But, dear Father, he is a worldly man, without any knowledge of Thyself or of the wonders of Thy Word.

"Do, I pray Thee, give me wisdom today. Set Thou a seal upon my lips and enable me to say only that which can be used of Thee that he may be saved."

She had ended the prayer, as was her wont, in Jesus' Name; and in the strength of that Name she had gone forth. Fownley had saved her from drowning and she in turn would rescue him from unbelief to a knowledge of Christ that his *soul* might be saved.

She knew now that she had been guided in her speech at his office and that her apparently harsh words had been directed from above. In the case of James Fownley, with his self-sufficiency, awakening must come startlingly, as a sort of mental explosion. "Like Naaman," she said to herself, "first 'mad' and then glad." Not that Fownley gave the impression of being always conscious of his own goodness but — to one of spiritual discernment — it was evident he was in love with himself and with his philosophy of life.

"I shall by the grace of God win him to Christ," she avowed, as she entered the dining room.

James was dining alone but she did not go to his table. Instead she smiled, nodded pleasantly and seated herself at a table in a far corner. He saw her smile and marveled, watched her furtively out of the corner of his eye. When she bowed her head in worship before eating, he was again moved with that same strange emotion which had stirred him that first morning.

"We're as far apart as the poles," he admitted soberly to himself. "She walks in the light of another world while I am still trying to find the light of this one." With this acknowledgment he set his cup of coffee down hard in its saucer and shrugged his shoulders.

In his room later he studied his face in the mirror. "Inconstant fool!" he labeled himself. "Trying to commit suicide because of one woman, and within a week's time leaning like the tower of Pisa toward another."

This last thought came as he caught the reflection of that ancient wonder in the picture on the opposite wall of the room. He turned and crossed the room, stood pensively studying this "Wonder of the World."

Less than two weeks ago he had purchased this painting and had it hung upon the wall.

He read again the description of it given below: "Built 1154 A. D. at Pisa, Italy, by Romano Pisano and William of Innsbruck, was intended to stand upright. But the soil gradually gave way on one side until the marble structure was 16 feet out of perpendicular."

The last sentence brought forth a smile, as for a brief minute he thought of June and her simple faith in God. "The foundation is now being reinforced by direction of Premier Mussolini."

But with the smile a stab of remorse went through his heart. For he, too, had once "stood," like Miss Darle, in matters of theology. "As straight as the New Testament," he said to himself. But now in this sense also he was leaning. "And it is too late to strengthen the foundations." Yet a sigh of wistfulness escaped his lips as he uttered the words.

But James did not know of June's determination to make him "stand" again nor that Another, great and mighty, had conspired with her, at her request, to set his feet forever on solid rock.

CHAPTER IX

It was late on a Saturday night. The pastor of Calvary Church was in his study, deeply engrossed in sermon preparation for the morrow. His face was marked by deep concern, yet a radiance shone there which revealed the sublimity of his thoughts. Tomorrow he would face an audience of eager listeners, men and women from many walks of life. Sunday after Sunday they came to hear him: the weary, the disheartened, the weak, the strong, all hungering for the one thing — the Bread of Life. He felt the tremendous weight of his responsibility.

Open before him on his desk was his study Bible, its pages well worn. Many of its precious truths were underscored. Other books, too, were there, as though he had searched widely for material suitable for the message of tomorrow.

For a moment he leaned back in his swivel chair and closed his eyes in relaxation. It would soon be time to retire. Mrs. Warburne had long since gone to her room.

The moment of quietude past, he opened his eyes and leaned forward to complete his work.

He was suddenly jarred from his meditations by the ringing of the door-bell. He had placed a silencer on the bell itself so that in case it should ring at this hour of the night — and it often did — his wife would not be disturbed. She had not been well in the past year and he was careful in the little things to safeguard her health.

The minister sighed. It was not easy to leave the things of the Spirit. His brow clouded for a moment as the bell rang again before he could reach the door. Perhaps someone was in distress. He quickened his step and opened the door at once.

He was greeted by a smooth, yet rapid voice of the middle register as his caller entered: "Good evening, Uncle Frederick — glad to see me? You are, aren't you?"

The newcomer closed the door behind him. The minister shook hands with him with as much warmth as he could command. It was evident he was not overjoyed by this visit. "Come into my office, Graig," he requested, "where our conversation will not be so likely to disturb your Aunt Margaret. She is not so well, you know."

"Yeah, I know — the old girl always did work too hard." His uncle frowned at the insult, but kept his peace. He was anxious to get back to his task.

Graig seated himself in the chair his uncle indicated, the fingers of his left hand thumping nervously on the desk.

"Well?" the minister began.

"Shall I come straight to the point?"

"The sooner the better, Graig."

"All right, I want one hundred dollars — I *have* to have one hundred dollars tonight."

The minister fixed his eyes soberly on his nephew as if to look straight through him.

"Tonight, eh? You mean this morning. It's past midnight." Graig shrugged.

"Gambling again? Can't you ever learn that the fool and his money are soon parted? What would your mother say —?"

"Leave her out of it."

"You remember her dying request that —"

Graig rose to his feet. "I remember nothing of the sort," he growled. Then, "Are you going to help me or not? If not, say so, and I'll get out."

The elder Warburne reached for his pocketbook. "Under one condition, Graig. Promise that?"

Graig's face relaxed and he sat down again, this time on the edge of his chair, while he leaned forward watching his uncle's movements. "I'll promise anything, only give me the money quick."

Again his uncle smiled. He knew the young man before him, had more intimate knowledge than the other guessed of his escapades. "Very well, then." His voice was steady and forceful. "You will attend my church tomorrow night."

The nephew scowled. "I'd rather eat soap," he said, "but I'll do it if you won't train your guns on me."

But his uncle was not through. "Graig," he said, gravely, his hand on the other's shoulder. "I am not going to give up on you until you are saved, and if it becomes necessary to have you put in jail first, I'll do that. I've stood about all I can. Your road is the broad road, son. I warn you that you are bound to reap the whirlwind sooner or later. God only knows what things you do that would make the angels shudder. The Devil is a hard master, Graig, and he will pay in his own coin. I may be doing someone a wrong by letting you have this money tonight."

He paused while his face suddenly softened. Then he said, tenderly, "Good night, Graig, and may God bless you!"

The other shrugged. "No danger of that."

When Graig had gone the minister stood for a moment in the center of the room, then he went quietly to his office where he closed the door and dropped to his knees. He did not pray long, for he was very tired, and he knew that the Heavenly Father understood. He tarried only long enough to cry out of a heavy heart for the soul of Graig Warburne, the only son of his brother Robert, who had passed away five years ago.

Graig hurried down the steps to a waiting cab and gave directions in low tones to the driver. When he was inside he opened his bill-fold and carefully tucked away the one hundred dollars.

The driver seemed familiar with the section of Oakland to which he was taking his passenger. In fifteen minutes he reached his destination and Warburne alighted. The driver watched him until he disappeared inside a softly lighted doorway. He knew the place for what it was, one of Oakland's elite gambling dens.

Warburne's entrance was greeted by silence. Two flashily dressed men came forward and seated themselves at a table on which lay, face down, a deck of regular playing cards.

Warburne took the remaining chair and with an expressionless face drew out his purse and handed over fifty dollars in bills. The hand of the man at his right reached for it. "Thanks, Graig," he muttered, "I'll be frank with you, I didn't think you'd be back tonight."

Warburne grinned. "Have I ever lied to you?"

The other grunted. "Well, no, not exactly. Although we've had to wait a week or two sometimes to find out whether you were telling the truth, eh, Blowers?"

Blowers assented, adding ironically, "And we've had to use pressure sometimes to keep the truth from being a lie."

And so the game began. The hours crept by and Graig's money dwindled slowly away. Then suddenly as if luck had changed Warburne began to win. His spirits revived and in less than half an hour he had won back all he had lost and more. He would have played longer but it was nearly four o'clock in the morning, time for closing.

The man named Blowers said something that aroused Graig's attention sharply. They were taking a last drink before leaving: "Say," he said, "I saw the swellest dame the movies ever put on the screen, tonight. Yes, sir, the show was on at the World Theatre — a revival of that picture 'Love for Three.' The girl was Mary Silvers. Remember her? The girl who disappeared from Hollywood last year? Say, that dame should've been made a star."

Warburne's face was a study. At the mention of Mary Silvers he started, regaining his composure with difficulty. A few seconds later he asked, casually: "Anybody know what became of her? Or why she left Hollywood?"

The other returned, "Nobody seems to know, but *baby!* Those eyes! As blue as indigo! And lashes? . . . as long as your fingernail! There was *one* brunette that outclassed all the blondes that anybody ever glorified."

When Graig arrived at his apartment he was exultant. He had had good luck tonight.

"A fool and his money are soon parted." He grinned with satisfaction. "Just so the other fellow is the fool."

He had, however, taken one drink more than he had intended and his thoughts were rather jumbled. Sleep, too, was about to overcome him.

He undressed and shuffled into bed. "Mary Silvers!" he said aloud. "Ho, ho, ho! Just the lady I was looking for! Mary Silvers! So June Darle thought that she could fool me, did she? Well, she won't always have a telephone near."

A few moments later he was asleep.

Meanwhile his two companions were discussing things not intended for Warburne's ears.

It was Blowers who spoke first. He waited until he was sure they were alone, then he signaled his companion to come nearer. Drawing from his vest pocket a ring he held it for a moment in the palm of his hand. "Look at this, will you?"

"What is it?" the other questioned, leaning forward.

Except for the proprietor they were the only two persons left in the long room.

"A diamond ring, a genuine diamond, and a beauty — it's worth hundreds! And it's too big for me."

The other looked at Blowers' thin fingers. "Where'd you — find it?"

"Last Sunday night, over in Oakland park."

"Did the park have any scruples against handing it over? — Man! look at it sparkle! "

"None whatsoever. It was a religious 'park' and just as meek and docile as a dime store lamb."

"Um hm, well?"

"I'm going to give it to Warburne."

"You're crazy!"

"Mmm — maybe not. This ring is marked inside with the owner's initials. I'm expecting the cops to be on the lookout for the fellow who — ah — found it, see?"

"Go ahead, I'm tuned in."

"Well, it's our chance to — well, help Warburne get on more intimate terms with the police."

"Come on, make it snappy, I don't see a bloomin' thing in the bushes, so you can quit beatin' around 'em!"

"O.K., boy. Here's how: We'll let him win it the next time we play. After that we'll start the whispers going. The guy who owned a ring like this has already told the coppers, you can bank on that."

Warburne, oblivious to any plot against him, slept soundly, awakening only when the church bells rang at eleven o'clock in the morning.

CHAPTER X

Mary Silvers sat in an easy chair gazing dreamily out of the window of her room. Before her in the distance rolled the waves of San Francisco Bay. The setting sun was partly hidden behind rose tinted clouds.

"Is there anyone here who is not prepared to enter the Golden Gate?" The words of the old hymn came singing into her heart as she meditated, her eyes drinking in the beauty of the sunset. To the left, dimly outlined against the horizon, lay the city of San Francisco. To the right and on the opposite side of the Bay from the city, purple hills rose gently in the shadow of towering Mount Tamalpais. In between lay the Golden Gate; beyond, the mighty Pacific.

Several weeks had passed since the night when she had been rescued from death. They had been happy weeks and truly the angel of the Lord *had* "encamped round about her." A Bible lay open in her lap. An underscored passage fixed her attention for a moment. It was the same verse that had sustained her throughout the past weeks. Again she lifted her eyes to the glowing sky. The message of the Book seemed to harmonize with the majesty and beauty of the vista before her. And even as this thought held her for a moment, there came another: a vision of the face of June Darle. It was June who was responsible for this happiness, who had made it possible for her to enjoy the beauty of a sunset and who had first showed her the greater beauty of knowing the Designer of all sunsets.

There was a gentle knock at the door. Mary responded with a quiet, "Come in." She did not rise, for she recognized the knock and knew that the one who would enter would not want her to do so.

She raised her eyes and smiled, holding out her hand in welcome. There were no words of greeting, the solemn majesty of the scene before them forbidding speech.

For a long while the silence continued. It was Mary who spoke first, her words coming softly: "Another week of this and I'll be entirely well again."

"I'm so glad for you," her companion returned, her voice composed and restful. "It has been so wonderful to have you here."

"And wonderful to have known you, Mother Tilden." She patted the hand which reached out to clasp hers.

"You'll be going to see your own mother soon, I suppose," Mrs. Tilden ventured. June had told her as much as she knew of Mary's story.

The other sighed. "I hope so, but —" She paused, biting her lip. "If I only dared, but I'm afraid."

"Afraid?"

"No — not of Mother, one couldn't be — of her . . . but of how the people will talk and act. There's no welcome for the prodigal girl; no, I think I shall never go home again."

Her companion was quiet for a long time after that. Then she said, softly, "Your mother loves you, Mary — doesn't she?"

Again there was silence. When at last Mary answered, her voice was hesitant: "I wish I could know for sure — you see, I ran away. I wanted the gay life, the thrills and the bright lights. Oh, I shouldn't have gone, but I wanted to try my wings — I didn't know then how easily wings are singed and — and how hard it is for them to heal." Her hand felt the sympathetic pressure of that of her friend.

"But now you know, dear?"

"Yes — even to the singeing of the wings," Mary said, sadly.

"And also to the healing of them."

"Perhaps — oh, I hope so. But I don't think I'll ever fully recover from it all: the gaiety, the glamour, and then the black, bitter disillusionment — it's almost too much to hope for that."

"But you still have your voice, Mary girl, and now that you have a new song —"

Mary sighed again. "Some day, perhaps. It's so good now just to have you and — rest."

The sun had disappeared, leaving a train of golden clouds and sky above the glimmering waters of the bay.

In the near foreground was the University campus, dimly visible in the twilight, the tall white tower of the Sather Campanile silhouetted against the rose and crimson of the west.

"Tomorrow," Mary said, "I should like to stroll through the campus."

Mrs. Tilden was glad to hear those words. It was the first time Mary had showed any desire to go beyond the garden.

When "tomorrow" came and the morning had passed and the afternoon sun had sent its silver rays into her room, Mary was ready for her walk. In the library downstairs sat Harwood Glover, Fownley's assistant in the book store, waiting for her to come down. Mrs. Tilden sat opposite him, smiling to herself as she reflected that June had used discretion in her choice of an escort for Mary. Early this morning the arrangements had been made.

"I'm so sorry I can't come, Mary," June had explained to her. "But I'm going to send you a friend, a very fine young fellow from the University — just a big overgrown boy. I've already adopted him for my brother. He'll show you about the campus and bring you home safely."

"I'll trust you, June," Mary had assured her. "If you'd send me out with a confirmed crook and tell me he was trustworthy, I'd believe you. But remember I've been bored to death with sheiks and philanderers. I shouldn't go an inch if I thought he'd try to make love to me."

It was a typical California day, the afternoon sun lavishing its warm caresses everywhere. The city of Berkeley was beautifully located between the hills and the Bay. The Tilden home, from its location on the hill slope, looked off across the expanse of city below to the Bay itself and on to the Golden Gate.

The white stone buildings of the University glistened magnificently in their setting of eucalyptus and oak trees, midst sweeping landscapes and well-tended lawns.

Mary smiled when she saw the bright red hair; and Glover smiled in return, taking Mary into his heart at a glance.

"Be sure to be back by five-thirty," Mrs. Tilden reminded them as they were leaving.

In due time they reached the campus, where Glover was immediately at home, pointing out the various buildings and places of interest: the open air Greek Theater, the Memorial Library, the towering Sather Campanile and the California Memorial Stadium.

"Miss Silvers, we have some of the biggest football games in the world right here, and believe me, we're going to trim U.C.L.A. so badly the next time they won't know what hit 'em."

Mary smiled. Without realizing she was doing so she began to tell him about the happy girlhood days back in her home town where life was simple and good and where friends were abundant.

"I've always wanted to finish college," she said, wistfully, "but I suppose it's too late now."

They strolled east to Bancroft Way, and at College Avenue turned north again.

"And here's good old Strawberry Creek — the south branch," Glover exulted, his face lighting up. Often he had followed its course, listening to its singing waters as it twisted its way, snake fashion, through the campus.

Mary stood near the stream, in her eyes a far-away look.

"A stream like this makes a fellow think, doesn't it?" he asked, as he read her face.

"All nature is like that," she replied, soberly. "One needs to get out in the open more, away from the noise and bustle and the false glitter of things, to feel the depth and the bigness of — life," she finished, still pensive.

For a moment Glover thought of June Darle as he studied her profile. All he knew of Mary was what June had told him: "A sweet girl who needs rest and quiet and — faith, Mr. Glover, and I want you to help me to help her find them."

"Yes, I certainly like old Strawberry Creek. Some day I'm going to take the canyon trail and see if I can find its source. It starts away up yonder in the hills somewhere and comes leaping and dashing down. Then it dives into its long culvert and is known no more until it comes out again here — runs right under Memorial Stadium! But here it is again, the same old creek, just as happy as ever, although not running quite so fast as up in the canyon."

Mary listened, her eyes wide and her thoughts still far away.

He checked himself. Had he talked too much and too enthusiastically? He had sought to keep his voice calm but his earnestness had almost run away with him.

Then Mary spoke slowly, "Life *is* like that, only when it finds a culvert, where it disappears — and when men play games above it while it runs silently on in the darkness — sometimes," she sighed, "sometimes it's not the same when it comes out into the sunlight, do you think?"

He was silent, guessing that she might be thinking of her own life, and afraid lest, if he speak, he might snap the thread of her thoughts.

At last he spoke, remembering June's request, "If a mere stream can keep on running, *after* the darkness, perhaps the river of life, with —"

He hesitated, somewhat embarrassed, yet feeling the urge within him to speak. "With *faith* we could do it, too, I should think. Old Strawberry seems to be all the grander when he comes marching out from under the Stadium. Anyway, I like him just as well — almost better."

The afternoon passed and Mary returned to her room to watch another sunset and to meditate anew upon the thoughts that had challenged her.

CHAPTER XI

Graig Warburne was preparing to attend the evening church service. With an eye to the future, he was going to keep his promise. Carefully he adjusted his tie and examined his profile, smiling with approval at the man in the mirror.

"A fool and his money! eh?" he laughed to himself. "Well, who's the fool? I wonder what old Religious would say if he knew I had ten thousand dollars in cold cash all salted down?"

It was still early. He would have time to stop at the Walhurst for Marlyn. An unpremeditated curse escaped his lips, followed by a whistle of exclamation. "Why not?" he said aloud.

Turning, he went to a secret hiding place in his bedroom and took out a thousand dollars in large and small bills. Tonight would be as good a time as any. With confidence stamped upon his face he hurried to the Walhurst.

Marlyn, arrayed in her newest and most ravishing gown was lounging on the divan in her room. Twilight had crept slowly in until it was now almost dark. Her thoughts were far from pleasant and she was desperately lonely.

Her attempts during the past week to win back Fownley had not been successful and she was deeply chagrined. She had an insatiable desire to smoke, but forbade herself that pleasure. She was hoping James would call for her. If to win him she must break the habit she would do so, at least until she had won him.

Thus Graig found her. Upon entering he held out his arms, but she eluded him.

"Don't, Graig dear, please — not tonight."

He stopped abruptly, annoyed. "You're lovely, gorgeous," he said. She had snapped on the lights when he entered.

"I'm glad you think so." The inflection was on the word "you".

"Aha! Fownley again, eh? Well, why didn't you marry him? Why don't you do it yet?" His tone was sarcastic.

Marlyn had had no intention of letting him know that her heart had returned to James; but she could not resist the temptation to cause him pain. "I would . . . if I could."

He laughed. "That's killing! . . . the most beautiful woman in the city unable to have her own way." He offered her a cigarette.

"No, thanks, I've quit."

He stared. "Oh! I forgot you'd been rubbing wings with an angel. How volatile some people are! How easily swayed by the religious! By the way, that reminds me, I have to go to church tonight — promised Uncle Frederick I'd do it; and incidentally I salted down a little dough. Go with me, Marlyn? Come on. Now that you've quit smoking you might just as well start going to church."

Marlyn's lip curled, "Go to church! Not till I'm carried in."

But in the end Graig won, and Doctor Frederick Warburne had at least two persons in his audience who seriously needed his sermon.

From their seat in the right wing of the balcony, Graig and Marlyn surveyed the vast throng that completely filled the church.

A cynical smile overspread Graig's features, while a feeling almost of jealousy swept over him.

Marlyn leaned toward him and whispered: "I didn't know so many young people ever went to church. There seem to be hundreds of them. I wonder if they're University students."

"If they are, I'll bet they're freshmen. Biology and Comparative Religions'll knock the church bug out of them in due time. I've got my eyes opened. I . . . ."

He was interrupted by the wave of silence which swept over the audience as the pastor arose for the beginning of the service. The organ ceased and the reading of the Scriptures began. The voice of the minister was clear and challenging: "For the god of this age (Satan) hath blinded the eyes of them that believe not."

Resentment swirled in the mind of Graig as he decided that the passage had been selected especially for him. The remainder of the Bible passage fell on closed ears and he cursed under his breath. He did not appreciate the beauty of the service nor the stirring appeal of the sermon. The eager, tense faces of the audience angered him. When he left the church the one scripture verse was ringing in his ears: *"For the god of this age hath blinded the eyes of them that believe not . . ."*

After the service he hailed a cab and drove with Marlyn to his apartment where two other couples joined them. An evening of cards, cocktails and garrulity, however, did not silence the voice of the Word in his soul.

It was two o'clock in the morning when he finally left Marlyn at her hotel. "May I come in for a moment, Marlyn?" he requested.

When they were alone he let out a deluge of curses that even Marlyn shuddered to hear.

"I wouldn't have heard what I've had to listen to tonight for five thousand dollars!" he exploded. "That's the curse of having had Christian parents! Bah!" He shook his head and shrugged his shoulders as if to hurl aside an unwanted presence. "Every time I start to do a thing I really want to do, that conscience of mine stabs me in the heart; and after I've done the thing it glares at me and points at me an accusing finger!"

Again he cursed the memory of his parents and paced the floor in a rage.

Marlyn watched him, a smile playing about her lips. Then she laughed. "Wonderful!" she exclaimed. "I like you when you're like that — so big —" Her voice began its favorite coo — "So grand and fierce. Do it again, Graig; I love it!"

He stopped and glared at her. "You think I'm acting?" he stormed. "Well, I'm not; I'm sore!"

"And you're *grand* when you're that way. You almost make me love you again — when you're like that."

He was cooling off now and his voice changed: "Listen, Marlyn, that's all right, you stick to Fownley." He paused, "What I really wanted to tell you is something else. I want you to do something, something with big money in it, see?"

"Yes, I see." She fixed her attention on what he was about to say. "And do I ever need more money!"

He drew out his wallet and counted five hundred dollars into her hand. "Enough?"

"For this month, yes."

He frowned and lowered his voice. "You're still showing June Darle around?"

"I am, although she goes out with Fownley a bit now."

He raised his eyebrows. Then his face darkened and his voice sobered. "Marlyn, there's serious business afoot and big money involved — lots of it, see?"

She nodded.

"Now here's all you need to do and all you need to know: Get as intimate as possible with this woman and find out from her — for me only, understand — what she knows about Mary Silvers and where she is. Mary used to be in the movies, you know. Find out where she is now . . . that's your job, and I don't care how you get your information. Only you must not, under any circumstances, let June know that I am interested. That's all."

He turned to go and then hesitated. "I'll tell you this much to whet your curiosity a little more: June Darle is not the only name your angel friend is known by."

Marlyn had her opportunity the next day. June had been planning for some time to spend a few hours watching the workmen who were engaged in the project of bridging the Golden Gate.

It was in 1919 that the feasibility of "bridging the Gate" was finally determined, but the problem of financing it had hindered any definite work. Permission, too, must be secured from the War Department, which finally gave its consent in 1924, since the bridge would be a positive military asset. After a long court battle, which ended in 1930, the legality of the project was announced and plans were formulated for the building of the bridge, whose center span was to be forty-two hundred feet, the longest suspension in the world. Now the actual construction was going on and June was eager to visit the scene of activity.

The gigantic towers rising on either side of the Gate would pierce the sky. The foundation of the south tower, on the San Francisco side, was now being built, an enormous caisson, the largest of its kind in the world. When completed it would be sunk twelve hundred feet off shore, where geologists had discovered that the rock formations were adequate. The erecting of this south tower presented the greatest difficulty. Here the flow of the tide is seven miles an hour and the water is always turbulent. Here, too, during storms the breakers are unusually high and the wind velocity sometimes attains to more than fifty miles per hour.

But the mind of man had conquered. By 1937 the six highway lanes of the bridge would be crowded with swiftly moving vehicles. All this June already knew. But she was amazed when they arrived at the access trestle to the south pier of Fort Point, the San Francisco approach. The stupendous undertaking held her speechless as arm in arm with Marlyn she watched the workmen.

"Suppose there should be a severe earthquake?" Marlyn queried. For a moment her eyes took on an expression of wonder. Left to her own choosing she would never have thought of finding anything to interest her in bridge building. Her life was that of a butterfly, flitting about only to sip the sweets of the flowers of this world. But in an unguarded moment she had actually allowed a constructive thought to enter her head. It seemed good to be able to think such a thought without having had someone else first suggest it.

June's answer was sober: "It would be serious if the bridge should go down while it was crowded with traffic."

A masculine voice at their left answered the question for them. "That bridge'll stand a bigger earthquake than has ever struck California. I . . ." the speaker was seized with a fit of coughing . . . "If you'll excuse me for interruptin'."

"Certainly," June assured him, "and thank you, too."

The man was flashily dressed.

"Yes, ma'am, you see this bridge'll be flexible on account of its being what they call the 'suspension type.' Although I reckon if an earthquake should split a hole in the bottom of the ocean right under the foundation of one of those towers there, it might upset things a bit."

June thanked him again, her tone bearing a note of dismissal. For, while she appreciated the volunteered information, she was aware of the rudeness of his manner of looking at them. Nor did she like his appearance.

But he did not catch her hint — at least he ignored it. He thought he knew women; and Marlyn's smile reassured him.

"Say, kid," he directed his words to Marlyn, "you're some swell looker. You make me think of a dame I saw at the theater the other night — Mary Silvers. Ever hear of her?"

Both Marlyn and June started at the mention of Mary's name.

"Mary Silvers?" Marlyn asked. "I believe I remember her, let me see . . ." She hesitated. Perhaps here was her opportunity.

"Yeah," the man put in confidentially, restraining his cough, which had started again. "She was a raving beauty with a swell chance to become a star . . . she played in that big sensation, 'Love for Three.' Remember?"

June was silent, pretending lack of interest.

Marlyn answered, "Oh, surely, I remember — I wonder what ever became of her. Didn't she disappear from Hollywood as if the earth had opened and swallowed her up?" Marlyn was rolling her eyes at him in the hope that thereby she might loosen his tongue and obtain the information she sought.

He grinned with approval at her boldness and replied: "Guess nobody knows that — anyway she's gone. Say, you needn't look so bored." He turned to June. "Maybe you know, yourself".

Marlyn broke in. "She knows almost everything, I can vouch for that. Don't you, June?"

"Not quite." June smiled. "I am not so well versed in the moving picture business. In fact I haven't attended a theater for several years."

"What!" his voice was incredulous. "Aw, come on, don't try to kid me!"

June met his gaze, not with challenging eyes as he had expected, but pityingly. She felt suddenly sorry for the bedizened youth before her, reading the emptiness of his soul and loathing the cheap and tawdry glare of his personality. She resolved to give him the reason why.

It was going to be hard to speak of spiritual things in this atmosphere. There were times, she told herself, that Christian tact would not allow her to do so. But, ever sensitive to the voice of the Spirit within, she knew that she must speak, must fling mere hesitation to the wind. *Ye shall be my witnesses,* was the sustaining word that girded her with courage.

"No," she repeated, and her voice was vibrant with sincerity. "I have not attended a movie since one glorious night years ago when — when I found something far better!"

He stared, speechless, held by the expression on her face.

June went on. "That was the night I became a Christian, when I opened my heart to the Lord Jesus Christ." When she finished, her soul was aglow and the light of it shone on her face.

Marlyn was plainly embarrassed as well as disappointed. She had hoped for some word from June in regard to Mary Silvers.

The young man continued, with his eyes upon June, "Say, you're a cute kid, where'd you get all that religion?" He was seeking to hide his embarrassment by a bantering tone. "Don't let me spoil your fun."

He rolled his eyes slowly at Marlyn and shrugged his shoulders. "Well, so long."

To himself he said, as he strode away, "Another one gone religious . . . not so bad lookin' though, and she sure looked like she meant what she said."

A little later June said to Marlyn, "It's not that a picture's wrong because it moves, nor that all who attend the movies are wicked, nor that every picture is evil in itself. But it's the whole corrupt business and what it does to the youth of our land: depraving their morals, robbing them of a love for the finer and better things and creating for them heroes and heroines from those who have no faith in God and very little, if any, appreciation of the sacred laws of marriage and of the home. Oh, it all makes me heart-sick! Sometimes I wish, desperately, that the whole thing would go completely bankrupt and be compelled to close down forever. When I think of what it does, not only to the patrons but to the actors and actresses themselves, it makes me shudder. There's Mary Silvers for instance —"

Although the conversation hovered near the place where Marlyn expected at any moment some revelation concerning Mary's whereabouts, she was disappointed.

They dined in the city; and after dark took the ferry for their own side of the Bay.

It was a cool night with salt breezes blowing from the sea. From the upper deck of the ferry they looked out over the waters. A friendly moon cast its silver shimmerings across the waves.

"It's been a lovely day, June, dear." Marlyn's voice was soft. "I'm so glad you let me go around with you, I get terribly lonely these days."

They were standing at the railing, facing the south. Only a few persons were on this side and none of them were near.

In answer June pressed her hand, warmly. "You do get lonely, don't you? Although you seem to have many friends and admirers."

Marlyn sighed. For a moment the contentment of her companion made her realize the restlessness of her own life, yet she did not believe that the secret of June's happiness could solve her own problems. "It isn't just admirers and friends that one needs." Her tone was wistful. "Sometimes one gets desperately lonely for something deeper . . . and more lasting."

"I know," June answered, softly, "admiration and mere friendship are like the summer months back East — they come and go. Our souls seem to need a climate like this out here: even when it's winter, it's still summer."

Again Marlyn sighed and her voice took on a plaintive note: "June, dear, there's something I've been wanting to tell you. Not that you'd be particularly interested or that I ought to tell you. But I can't help it. May I?"

"Of course." June felt drawn to this poor creature of the world and her heart ached for her that she might come to know the side of life that was rich and full, that meant more than imaginary pots of gold at the foot of an ever receding rainbow. Marlyn spoke once more and her tone was sad: "I've lost the only real love I ever had, I — I was to have been — married three weeks ago last Friday night but —" Her voice broke.

June's arm went around her in sympathy. Marlyn continued in more even tones, "But something has happened; I don't know what. You — you know him . . . James Fownley . . . oh, I don't think I can stand it to give him up!" Again her voice choked.

June recalled that same Friday night. That was the night that Fownley had saved her. A peculiar sensation overswept her. For some time she was silent, while thoughts flew swiftly through her brain.

Marlyn continued: "He has not been the same since that night. I don't know if there is another woman or what, but he ignores me — almost snubs me now."

A half hour later in her room, Marlyn studied her face in the mirror. "Sometimes, Marlyn, my dear," she crooned to herself, "I think you should be living in Hollywood. That was the grandest piece of acting you've done in a long time. June Darle'll have something to think about now. She knows *I* know she has been going out with him."

Before retiring she held James' picture under the light. "You'll be mine yet, James Fownley." For a moment her heart was tender as she pressed the picture to her lips.

In her own room June knelt to pray, "O Father, let me win him for Thee. Thou knowest I have had but one desire. Keep me, I pray, from all danger in these dark days and continue to use me in that for which I have come to this city . . . in Jesus' name, Amen."

But when she arose the next morning the words of her prayer were saying themselves over and over again in her mind, "I have had but one desire." Then in a moment of self-revelation there came to her a startling thought, "She *had* had but one desire — namely, to win him to Christ." But that one desire had been strangely augmented to include also a desire, as yet vaguely understood, *to win him for herself!* The memory of that night at the Bay returned and she felt herself once more in his arms . . . being carried. With the thought came a sweet, tender feeling of reverence which she cherished for a full moment; and then she sought to drive it from her mind.

CHAPTER XII

Things were happening to James' heart, too, as the weeks and months slipped by. It seemed that everything he did and every conversation was planned so that his thoughts were turned to June.

It was Tuesday, November 6, election day. Today would determine the destiny of thousands of office seekers throughout the nation. The political situation in California was attracting world-wide attention. Everywhere in the city and over the state the chief topic of conversation for months had been the sudden and phenomenal rise to popularity of the present governor's most dangerous opponent. As usual in political campaigns, the voting would be done more or less blindly. For there was little that either party could boast but that the other could easily "prove" that it was not for the good of the people.

Fownley, seated at the breakfast table in the Walhurst, scanned the columns of the morning paper. From one end to the other it was ornamented with photographs of office seekers, whose advertisements described in glowing paragraphs, profuse with adjectives, the sterling qualities of "the man you should vote for."

Grant Weston announced his presence by touching Fownley on the elbow. "Going to vote?"

Fownley looked up. "Waffles, bacon and coffee," he ordered. "Yes, I believe I shall."

"How you going to vote? Russian?" Grant was off with the order. When he returned James answered his question:

"I'm going to vote for the EPIC program if that's what you mean."

Grant shrugged, pursed his lips and raised his eyebrows. "Suit yourself, but if you ask my opinion, a program like that will never succeed in any single state. It'd have to be national to succeed. And then it would very likely be a flop. If we tried to put on a program like that we'd have nothing *but* poverty out here. The poor of all the other states would come in swarms;

73

and the rich would move out to a state where they could do as they pleased without being so heavily taxed. Of course if California wants to secede from the Union —"

"Listen, Grant," Fownley interrupted, "I'm voting for the 'End Poverty in California' campaign. In a few years — mark my word — something like this will be the issue in the whole of America. The man who rises to power will be the one who promises Utopia for his followers. Look at Mussolini, Hitler, Stalin and all the little dictators. They all posed as saviours first, didn't they? Well, that's what we need in this country — a saviour."

"How do you spell that word? With a capital 'S?' I see you're actually beginning to turn religious. Well —" Weston's tone was ironical. "I can't say that I blame you, I've been rather expecting it." He turned to leave but Fownley's hand stayed him.

"I asked you once before to leave out that kind of talk, Grant. That's my own business."

At the store he was greeted by Glover's usual cheery good morning and the customary torrent of words in regard to the morning's business. "Good morning, Mr. Fownley," he exclaimed, his red head bobbing about as he rearranged the books in the window. *"Mad World* is still going like griddle cakes. Sold fifteen to a Sunday School teacher this morning for her class. The lady said she wanted her young people to read about the sacredness of marriage and the need of both husband and wife being Christians — say, you know what? I've been reading the book myself, between customers, and it says that last year there was one divorce for every three marriages in the state of California."

Fownley was reminded that he had not as yet read the book. "Well, what about it?" His voice was almost abrupt.

"Oh, nothing!" Glover's spirits sank a notch or two at his employer's tone. "The book says — pardon me for quoting it so much — that there's only one way to solve the divorce question."

"Oh," Fownley grunted as he passed on to his office.

In his office James closed the door and turned to his morning mail. A small, white envelope, addressed in a smooth hand, received his first attention. Curiously he opened it, half expecting and vaguely hoping that it might be from June. Varied emotions stirred him and his hand trembled as he opened the envelope. The contents were brief. Only the date was given, no address. It was signed, simply "Mary."

James read:

"Dear Mr. Fownley:

"Since that night in the Knickerbocker I have wanted to write to you or see you personally. I rather feel that you were offended at what Miss Darle said about the book I bought at your store, and I wish to assure you that she was right. Please, oh please, Mr. Fownley, never sell a book like that without telling the purchaser what it is and at least warning him that it is deadly poison.

"You see, when one is at the point of desperation, only faith in a living, reigning God can help. I was spared the horrors of leaping into a Christless eternity — thanks to His faithful servant, June Darle."

The letter both startled and angered him. With a restive gesture he tossed the letter into the waste-basket. Then on second thought he recovered it and placed it in his inside coat pocket. He then proceeded to take care of all necessary business as quickly as possible. Glover would leave at 10:45 for his class at the University, which meant that he must go to the polls at once.

"I'll be right back," he said to Glover as he hurried out. It was now 10:30.

Arriving at the voting place a block away, he hurriedly entered the booth and marked his ballot. In his haste he did not notice the man who entered the booth immediately after he had left it. Nor was he aware that, reaching into his pocket for a slip of paper on which were written the names of certain persons for whom he wished to vote, he had drawn out a small, white envelope, unnoticed, and dropped it.

Graig Warburne was keenly disappointed that Marlyn had been unable to procure for him the information he sought. The weeks were slipping by and he was still looking in vain for Mary Silvers. He was in a particularly ugly mood this morning. In his anger and determination to attain his end, he knocked loudly at June's door. Receiving no response he concluded that she might have gone to Fownley's store; and immediately he proceeded thither.

Arriving at the Green Front Book Shop just as James was leaving, he followed him.

The curtain hanging in the doorway of the booth where James was voting did not reach to the floor. Consequently when the envelope fell from his pocket, Graig saw it at once. He turned when Fownley came out, and James, with his eye on his watch, did not see him.

Behind the curtain Graig stooped, picked up the letter and hurriedly marked his ballot. When he reached the street he inspected his find, cursing triumphantly to himself, as he read.

"Hm, I wonder." He reviewed in memory the conversation with June in the Knickerbocker that Sunday night. It was undoubtedly Mary Silvers who had been with June that night, although when he had returned the next day the clerk at the desk refused to give him any information. If it had not been for that telephone —! He set his jaw. "The little demon! This means an early interview with June Darle."

Stopping at the Western Union he seated himself at a desk and penned a message. When he had completed it he handed it to the young woman who came to receive it. "For a friend of mine," he explained, as she saw the signature.

"You're sure this is not your newly adopted alias?" she ventured, smiling.

"Sh!" he muttered, "keep that brilliance for more convenient seasons and keep your eyes open for a return message. You know my address. There'll be a change of address soon, but you won't need to worry."

She nodded. "You're paying for the telegram?" she asked, quietly.

He handed her a dollar.

"Is that all?"

He scowled, then pressed another bill into her hand.

"That's better." She smiled again. "This is dangerous, you know." Her voice dropped to a whisper as she heard the footsteps of a fellow employee coming from the rear.

"All right, sir," she said, pleasantly, and turned to tap out the message.

In the street Graig took a cab and rode to the Walhurst, where he learned that June had gone out for the day. She had left word that in an emergency she could be reached at a certain address. "It's not exactly an emergency, but I — she had an appointment with me," Graig lied.

It happened that on Tuesdays Giles Fallenby had the morning free from classes at the University, and was therefore on duty at the desk today. In his usual, indolent manner, he rose to his feet and towered above his questioner. "You're her brother, you say? Well, I'll give you her address." It was apparent that his mind was on something else and that, as usual for him, he was anything but alert. The only reasons he retained his position were his affable smile and his sudden capacity for being extraordinarily wide-awake whenever the manager put in an appearance.

As Warburne accepted the card on which was written the information he sought, Giles yawned, perceptibly. He had been on duty late the previous night and was still sleepy. "Say, Mr. — ah — Darle," he drawled, "what do you know about this?" He handed Graig a green-and-white-jacketed book. "You been following these kidnapping cases in the papers? Well, read this." He yawned again.

Impatiently Graig read: "Kidnapping for the purpose of extortion is now punishable by death in eleven states, as follows: Alabama, California —"

He stopped reading at the word California and shrugged his shoulders. In a disinterested tone he said, "Well, that serves 'em right; more power to the law."

When he had gone Giles resumed his reading, arousing himself only when someone approached the desk. At Marlyn's room Graig left certain instructions and a few minutes later was in a cab hastening toward his destination.

"Marlyn," he said, as he was leaving, "you'd better stay in your room pretty closely for a few days. You have a cold, see? And can't very well go out. Keep your eyes open and your mouth shut."

She nodded. "All right, Graig, old dear. Are you sure I have enough money for doctor bills — in case my cold gets worse or develops pneumonia or something?"

"If you don't have enough, charge it to me — confound you, Marlyn. I think *bigger* money would make you play false to me!"

She pouted at that and whimpered lackadaisically. "Oh, Graig, darling, you know that could never be." She seized him by the lapels of his coat and lifted her face close to his. "You know I love you, don't you? It's just that I need so much for clothes and things."

Nevertheless when he left, he believed that she would gladly play him false and that, somehow or other, Fownley was to blame.

CHAPTER XIII

In the hill district of the city the Tilden home nestled, restfully, on its gently rising slopes. Flowers of many kinds and colors nodded in the morning sun, lavishing their fragrance upon the breezes that whispered, softly, around the shrubs and orange trees.

June and Mary had found a little nook in the far corner of the garden, where, on a rustic, willow seat, they chatted of things of interest to them both.

Rising early, June had completed her morning correspondence and other duties and at ten o'clock was saying, "Good morning" to Mother Tilden. Mary was in her room.

"Come in, June," Mrs. Tilden welcomed her. "Just on time, to the very minute. Mary will be down soon."

June smiled. "And how is our girl?"

"Doing splendidly, happy and full of hope. Although at times she seems a little morbid. Her college friend has called a number of times and they laugh and chatter like a couple of children. I'm actually afraid the poor boy will neglect his studies, but he says not. He runs over sometimes when there's an hour between classes and they study together."

June was pleased. She knew the value of such friendships. Mary came down in a few minutes and together they strolled out to the garden.

Birds sang from the trees and flitted about. An occasional humming bird paused, suspended, and darted away again. Across the sloping lawn a neighboring garden surpassed in beauty even this one. In the midst of it, lying like a jewel in the palm of the hand, was a small lake. Shrubs, willows and other trees hugged its shores. Water fowl, swimming in its waters, sent little wavelets rippling across its otherwise placid surface.

"I find it easy to rest here," Mary was saying, musingly. "Everything is so peaceful and Mother Tilden is so kind. She reminds me of my own mother."

"You must have a precious mother."

"I have," Mary began, but stopped suddenly.

June had come today with a special purpose in view. She had written to Mary's mother, saying that she hoped to have good news for her soon. Today June desired to instill in Mary a longing to return to her home.

Mary spoke once more. There was something in her tone which made June remember what Mrs. Tilden had said about her moods.

"Yes, I have the dearest mother in all the world and someday, perhaps, I shall want to see her, but I — June — I'm afraid!"

June moved nearer and encased Mary's hand in her own. "Tell me," she said, "if you care to."

Mary's tone was sad as she replied, "I want to tell you — I wanted to tell Mother Tilden, too, but —" She bit her lip. "It's all so wonderful, to have all this kindness lavished upon me and to know that someone really cares and seeks for my happiness. It's wonderful, too, almost impossible to believe that — that Another cares and loves me, but —"

Mary paused again, her face shadowed with sorrow and anxiety. "It's the past, June, the awful, *terrible* past."

"But the past is gone forever."

"Oh no! no! if it only were, but it isn't. It keeps coming back to me: stark, hideous, haunting. . . . Sometimes I think I can't stand it, and then —"

"And then?"

"Then I remember the precious verse you gave me . . . in the Psalms. That helps, but when I think of going home, I — I just can't forgive myself. The old past looms before me and makes me afraid. Even of the future."

"But God forgives and blots out *everything*. When we truly believe on His Son, the blood of Jesus Christ cleanseth from all sin, all of it."

Mary shook her head. "Not all, surely."

"Yes, *all*. His Word is true." June drew from her purse her New Testament, found the verse she had just quoted and allowed Mary to read for herself.

Again Mary spoke, her voice subdued: "I want to tell you everything, June. You've been so good to me — such a friend. You'll let me, won't you? I just *have* to tell someone."

Again June pressed the hand of her friend. Mary was beautiful this morning, the sunlight playing upon her hair. But she looked sad, too. June was conscious that, even though she had been able to lead her to accept the Lord Jesus as her Saviour, Mary had not fully grasped the provision of Calvary for *all* sin. She must allow Mary to tell her story. Perhaps then she could open the Scriptures to her and make the way plain. A great love welled up in her heart for this girl. It had been growing more and more since the night they first met.

"You see," Mary began, "I not only ran away to Hollywood, but I also ran away to be married. My family hated him but he was so tall and handsome and made love so beautifully — promising me a career and fame — that I was completely carried away. When we arrived in Hollywood I was taken to the Superior Studios and given a personal introduction to the manager, who knew my husband — we were married, secretly, on the way out. At first there seemed to be a real chance for me and I was happy, playing in a few pictures as an 'extra.' But I wanted stardom. No one can be satisfied in minor roles when the ambition to become a leading lady burns in her breast.

"Then they gave me a chance to take a leading part in that picture, 'Love for Three.' I was elated when I saw myself on the screen.

"It was at this time that I awoke to the fact that my husband was already going about with other women. Then my health began to fail. I had been up too late nights; I had been on too many parties. The gay crowd, the cocktails, the cigarettes — all broke down my resistance. I laughed and played and tried to make myself believe that I was happy. But I wasn't. I wanted to be a star. I needed money, desperately, too. The company brought a statement for me to sign about the brand of cigarettes I used. I signed it. I was a veritable slave to cigarettes. Of course I could say they helped me act more naturally, for I had become so in bondage to them that I was not myself without them.

"My picture appeared in hundreds of newspapers throughout the country. Perhaps others had made such statements, sincerely, but I knew I had lied for publicity's sake. The company, of course, reaped the benefit, for 'Love for Three' was announced alongside the cigarette advertisement."

Mary stopped for a moment, then she resumed her story:

"They promised me a leading part in a picture to be made three months later and I was happy. Then began the long struggle. My salary had been much too small for our needs. The contract was signed for the big picture and I was being paid in advance, but my husband took the money as fast as it came.

"This was two years ago. At last I was unable to continue my work. The contract had to be broken. It was then that my husband disappeared entirely. Five months after that my baby was born — a beautiful baby." The tears suddenly came to Mary's eyes but she clenched her hands and continued:

"Let me tell you," she cried, "I *must* tell it! Two weeks later he — he *died!* I can remember the doctor's words now as he looked at me. I know he was sorry afterward that he had said it. But oh, he had told the truth. He said, looking at me very quietly and speaking gently:

" 'Your baby was poisoned.'

"I was horrified.

" 'Before it was born,' he said, gravely.

"I knew what he meant, for at that very moment I was lighting a cigarette. I couldn't rest until I searched the libraries and the latest medical journals, and his statements were confirmed. Not all babies born of cigarette-smoking mothers die, but more of them do than those whose mothers do not smoke. But I'm almost glad now that he didn't live. I couldn't have provided for him and he would have been without a father."

After a moment of silence June asked, tenderly:

"You never hear from your husband?" The story had awed her. Once more she had come face to face with one of life's dark tragedies.

"Once in the past year, and that was the news of his death. I came to Berkeley, thinking perhaps I could attend his funeral, but I became so desperate — you — you know the rest." Mary began to sob.

"Yes, Mary, I know, and I love you all the more. The past doesn't count, either to me or to our dear Lord. It says, 'All sin,' Mary, and it's all under the blood . . . forever: all your past and all mine. Even if you alone were to blame, rather than a sleeping society which allows all sorts of evils to flourish, even if mighty, moneyed interests were not also culpable, your forgiveness would be none the less absolute. Oh, I praise Him for the cleansing blood! Don't you? One almost wants to shout the words of that matchless old hymn: 'Hallelujah, What a Saviour!'"

"But I cannot forget. I keep thinking of that precious little face and the tiny hands. No wonder I hate the very sight of a cigarette!"

"But the Blood cleanseth, Mary."

"Yes," Mary breathed, and her face shone in the light of a new understanding.

Thus the Heavenly Father fortified the heart of his child against the severe trials that were just ahead. For no sooner had the precious truth of her complete forgiveness dawned upon Mary than the dark cloud of a new sorrow swept suddenly across the horizon. June had excused herself for a moment that she might assist Mrs. Tilden in the preparation of the noon meal, leaving Mary alone in the garden.

Suddenly a voice spoke from behind the bench: "Good morning, Mary Silvers Warburne! Aren't you glad to see your husband, my dear?"

Mary turned and sprang to her feet, her eyes taking on an expression of horror. "Graig!" she cried, and fainted in his arms.

"Fine! Splendid!" he exulted, as he lifted her. "Jove, if I don't like your golden hair! I hardly knew you."

Quickly he carried her to a waiting cab and drove away.

Twenty minutes later Graig and Mary were in his apartment. Mary was sitting with her hands clasped tightly together, watching him as he moved about, fear and horror on her face.

"Well, Mrs. Warburne." He stopped before her. "You thought you could hide from me, didn't you? Didn't you know that I'd never allow my beautiful wife to escape me?"

She was silent, her trembling hands clinging tightly to a little Testament June had given her in the garden.

"Answer me!" he demanded. "Didn't you realize I'd search till I found you?"

"I didn't run away from you — ever. You left me to starve — me and my baby!"

A shadow of anger crossed his face. "Forget that stuff!" he growled, and shrugged his shoulders. "You broke the movie contract and lost our chances of becoming millionaires."

She was silent. "We won't discuss it, Graig."

"Oh yes, we will!" He set his face and moved a step nearer, his eyes fierce, menacing. "We'll discuss that and other things. You're my wife — Mary Silvers Warburne: And *I'm* your husband! Look at me!" he demanded.

Mary lifted her eyes to his.

"You broke the contract," he insisted, stubbornly.

"And *you* broke my heart, Graig, and my spirit! I couldn't go on after that. Besides, I wasn't well."

He shrugged as if to dismiss any thought of his guilt. "What made you dye your hair?" he demanded. "So you could hide from me?"

"I thought perhaps as a blonde I'd have a better chance to find work. Besides I wanted to — forget."

"To forget *me!*" He glared at her.

"Yes, I tried to do that, too. I — I still loved you, then — until something died in me. When I saw the notice of your death, I was moved again. I spent my last penny to come here. I — I thought I wanted to see your face once more —"

"You wanted to see me *dead!*" he hurled at her, mercilessly.

She ignored the thrust and continued, "I lost heart after I got here and I decided to go to my own funeral instead."

"Well, why didn't you?"

Mary's face lit up and she lifted the little Testament and held it, proudly, triumphantly toward him. "This is why!" she cried, exultantly. Her voice was suddenly vibrant with courage. "Someone who believed this Book saved me! And now I not only live, but I live *eternally!* It's wonderful, Graig."

His arms gestured in angry impatience. "Stop it!" he cried. "Has everyone taken up this crazy religion? I'll make June Darle pay for this!"

"You know her? Oh, she's marvelous."

"Cut it out, I tell you!" Impulsively, he stooped and seized the Testament, tearing it in pieces. "I want you to forget this religious rot! Do you understand?"

Mary shrank from him. It seemed that in the loss of the book she had been robbed of her only weapon of defense. Suddenly she was afraid — desperately afraid of him. Terror seized her and she rose and fled to the door, frantically trying to open it and crying, "Help! help!"

But he was upon her in a moment, with his hand over her mouth to stifle her screams. He dragged her back into an inner room.

"Why don't you pray?" he sneered. Then he stood and laughed, as she stood before him, silent.

"And now!" he said, his breath coming heavily, "you'll grant a special request which I have to make."

He brought pen and paper and placing them before her, demanded, "Write what I tell you."

When she realized what it was he wanted her to write, Mary refused.

"Listen, Mary!" he thundered. "You write what I tell you or —" He paused. He knew she would never do it for her own sake. "For your Bible-believing friend's sake," he muttered, his jaw set and his eyes glaring, savagely. "I'll have her put out of the way within twenty-four hours if you don't."

Outside Blowers, flashily dressed, stood for a brief interval, scrutinizing the number of the apartment. For a moment a fit of coughing seized him. As he sauntered down the street in apparent unconcern, he said to himself:

"I'd know that girl if she had green hair! Hm! Mary Silvers being led into Graig Warburne's apartment by Graig himself. She didn't dare call for help but she certainly needed it! The dirty louse! He'll be in for it now — I won't even need to mention the ring. Just start the ball rolling along another line ... Hm! ... Everything is pretty well keyed up right now ... It's about time a good kidnap scandal got started." He quickened his step. "Well, here goes!"

CHAPTER XIV

June was in a quandary. Three days ago — the very afternoon of Mary's mysterious disappearance — she had received the peculiar letter which she now held in her hand. She could not believe what her eyes read:

"Dear June:

"Please forgive me for running away, but my husband who I thought was dead, came for me almost as soon as you went into the house. I have gone away with him. We are going to begin over. Please do not try to find me. I am writing to Mother today telling her not to worry. Promise me one thing, June dear: Do not communicate with Mother for at least another month. She does not know that I ever married and it would break her heart. As you love me, *please* grant my request in this. More than this I cannot tell you, except that my life has been threatened. My husband found out about it. He says it would mean instant death for me should my present whereabouts become known. (Psalm 37:4.)

"Always yours,
"Mary"

At this very hour in Lohengren, Nebraska, Mary's mother sat in her home, two telegrams and a letter in her lap. A smile was on her face.

The first telegram was dated Tuesday, November 6. It said, simply:

"EXPECT GOOD NEWS STOP DO NOT WRITE OR TELEGRAPH UNTIL NOTIFIED   (Signed)   JUNE DARLE"

The second was dated the same day in the afternoon and was a day letter. Mrs. Silvers read it once more:

"HELLO MOTHER DEAR I AM ALL RIGHT DON'T WORRY I EX-
PECT TO BE HOME IN A FEW WEEKS I CANNOT GIVE YOU MY

86

Mrs. Silvers' hand trembled as she turned to the letter. "My
Mary," she breathed, happily. "I'm going to see her again. Oh,
if it were only today!"

Again and again she read the precious words, lingering over
each endearing term. The last paragraphs she read aloud:

"And please forgive me, Mother dear, for writing with this
old typewriter. I fell yesterday and hurt my hand — not seriously, but I have it tied up and just can't hold a pen at all.

"Be sure to send me the money quickly. I hate to ask it,
but what else can I do? My check won't come from the
studios for three weeks and I simply have to have $3,000 at
once before I can clear up my debts to come home. Send it in
bills in an insured package. I don't like to cash checks in
strange banks. I'll pay it all back when I get home, Mumsy
dear. Don't forget my address: Parmeda, California, General Delivery.

"P. S.: You know how I feel about having run away from
home, so I'm asking you please not to tell anyone you're
sending me the money. It is nobody's business but ours. Also,
please, send it addressed to June rather than to me. M."

At ten o'clock the next morning an insured parcel lay in its
place in the post office ready to be dispatched to Parmeda, California.

Things were ripening for action on the Coast. The political
spree in which the Utopians, the Townsendites and other Old-
Age-Pensionites and their enemies had fought long and hard,
was over. The huge audiences that had gathered in numbers
aggregating 30,000 to 40,000 in the Hollywood Bowl had been
only the public manifestations of the private workings of the
hectic politicians and paradise hunters. Keyed to the acme of
expectancy, only to be disappointed, the crowd was incited to a
spirit of revenge. Where now could they turn to find new excitement? What new thing could they do to relieve the strain
of high-tensioned nerves?

And so it was that the kidnap scandal was welcomed. The general public remembered Mary Silvers, although the intervening years since she had disappeared had caused many to forget. Thousands read, avidly, the newspapers which said, "on good authority," that she had been seen struggling in the arms of a man — *being carried into a Berkeley apartment.* Thousands also flocked to the theaters to see her once more on the silver screen; and the theater management was glad for the free advertising.

Three days had gone by before the "news" had been reported, so that a letter and the parcel of money was already on its way to California before the actual scandal was started. An Oakland paper got the "scoop" and all articles were copyrighted. The source of the information was kept "secret" in order to protect certain "informants." The name of the kidnapper was not made known, although it was reported "on good authority" that the police knew their man.

June believed that her loyalty to Mary must lead her to keep quiet as to the letter she had received. When the first flaming headlines of the papers flung their startling news to a gaping public, she had felt constrained to go straight to police headquarters and tell all that she knew. Yet when she remembered the request of the letter she was restrained. Calling a cab she drove at once to Mrs. Tilden's home, where she received her pledge of silence. Then rushing to Fownley's book store she went into conference with Glover, who happened to be alone in the shop at the time.

"Let us keep absolutely quiet for a few days," she requested, earnestly.

Glover was tense with excitement. The times which he and Mary had spent together held for him happy memories and he had come to have a deep respect and tenderness for her. He felt a righteous pride in the fact that he had had a part in helping her to regain a new self-respect and he hoped he had helped her to believe — a little more at least — in God and in His Son, Jesus Christ. His first impulse was to take the best clue he could find and follow it until he hunted down the kidnapper.

June watched the manifestations of conflicting emotions on his face. She wondered if Mary had told him of her husband,

and concluded that she had not, for, as she saw the look of pain
in his eyes, she guessed that already there had developed in his
heart a deeper feeling for her than mere friendship. She dared
not disillusion him. Instead, she said, "Mr. Glover, I want you
to promise me to say nothing about this matter until I give you
the signal. I — you see, I've had a letter from Mary — no, I
don't have it with me. She says her life is threatened. The
very minute her whereabouts become known — nobody knows
what may happen."

His jaw dropped as he stammered, "I — I promise."

Fownley, too, was moved strangely by the news of Mary's
alleged kidnapping. Several times within the past few days he
had noted the care-strained expression on June's face. He hoped
she would permit him another interview soon.

This morning as he hurried to his store, her last words to him
were revolving over and over in his mind.

"I could learn to care for you, James, but I dare not let myself." Her eyes had said more than that. Yes, they had declared, unmistakably, "I love you *now,* but I must not — I dare
not let my heart have its way."

He had hoped that the time might come soon when he should
hear her say in words what her eyes had already revealed. In
the ardor of his own love, he had replied, "If you can learn to
love me, then I shall teach you — even against your will . . .
May I?"

"No," she had said, with finality, "I can only be your friend."

Her handshake was warm and almost lingering as they parted.
Fownley cherished the emotion that it had incited and he was
filled with a glad hope. The stars had never seemed brighter
than on that night.

Sitting on the edge of the very pier where they had first met,
they talked in low tones, recounting the events of that first night
and of other things that had happened in the intervening weeks
and months. It was a dangerous place for James and he knew it.
His love for Marlyn seemed to have died completely. He wondered now that he had ever cared for her. The memories of the
night when he had carried June in his arms were precious. It
was she who had saved his life, for in rescuing her, he had

driven from his mind forever the thought of suicide. Yes, he owed his life to her. He wondered, had it been anyone other than June Darle would the effect on him have been the same? Could any other woman have moved him to want to live? Recalling the despair of that hour and the awful mania that had overmastered him, he doubted it.

Yes, this was a dangerous place. With an almost mad yearning he wanted to pour out to her the story of his love and to take her once more in his arms, when she would be, not cold and limp as on that other night, but responsive to his embrace.

Instead, however, he forcibly contented himself. The moon was sailing low. "June," he said, his voice husky, "do you think you could learn to care for me in the way you know I want you to?"

It was then that she had given him the answer. That was last week. Since then they had not been together, and since then had come election day and the disappearance of Mary Silvers. On that day, too, he had lost the letter Mary had written him.

Now as he entered the block in which his store was located he wondered if the letter had been found. Had it had anything to do with Mary's kidnapping? It occurred to him that he should report the loss of that letter to the police, but with the thought came also a realization of the folly of such a procedure, for it would involve June also.

Thus, as on that night when he had gone to June's room to talk with her about the Bay suicide, he now felt that he should see her once more. He must tell her about the letter.

When he entered the store and found her in conversation with Glover he was glad, although he trembled inwardly with that innate fear with which lovers are sometimes afflicted. When they were alone in his office he began the conversation by saying:

"I received a letter from Miss Silvers."

June was immediately alert.

"On election day," he explained, "the day she is supposed to have been kidnapped."

June waited for him to continue.

"There was no hint in it that anything had happened. It merely expressed her deep appreciation for you and included a pretty stiff sermon for me — which I am taking somewhat seriously," he added soberly.

"Did she tell you of her new joy?" June began, suddenly aware that James did not believe and therefore could not fully appreciate the fact of Mary's having become a Christian.

He answered, "She said you were right that night about the book, *De-throning God,* and insisted that it gave her courage to try to end her life." His voice was respectful, bearing none of the spirit of irresponsible braggadocio which had been manifest in their first interview here months ago. He continued, "June, I have almost concluded that she is right. At any rate I've had the book taken from our list."

June's face brightened. "I admire you for that. Some day something else will happen to you — some day I shall call you 'brother.' "

He waved his arm as if in impatience. "You know I could never be satisfied with that." His eyes were betraying him again. He sought to regain his aplomb. "June," he said, "I haven't forgotten that night last week, and I swear to you that some day I am going to hear you say —"

"Don't, James — not today, please."

"But you *do* love me?" he demanded hopefully.

"Even if I did it wouldn't matter. I could never marry you — never!"

"There's someone else!" he cried, jealousy oversweeping him for the moment.

"No."

"Then why?" He had risen and was standing before her.

June thought he had never looked so manly and fine. She felt the power of his nearness. Desperately she planned the words for her reply and bravely she uttered them: "I've told you before," she said. Her tone bore a note of finality which belied her eyes.

"You mean the 'unequal yoke'?" His voice was incredulous.

"Yes."

"But June, my dear." He took her hands and raised her to her feet, the agony of his eyes crying out to her his love. He had never loved a woman like this before, he was sure. He felt, suddenly, that he must hear her say "yes" today. He found his voice again, "Love, June — true love — is the voice of God, is it not? If our love is mutual, then — then surely there could be no higher authority."

She allowed her hands to remain in his. "There is His own revealed Word," she said, finding new courage in speaking. "I know no higher authority than *that*. His Precious Word says, James, 'Be not unequally yoked together with unbelievers.' I've staked my life — my whole eternity — on the Book!"

He released her hands, seeking to read in her eyes some evidence that she would yield; but he saw in them only her desire to yield, and, man that he was, he would not press her now. Yet he knew he must express in words the thought of his heart.

"June," he said, "I shall not give you up until I have — no, I shall *never* give you up! I cannot believe that the fact that you are a believer — a Christian — and that I am a skeptic has any right to keep us apart. To me the highest law in the universe is the law of love. If that is not God's way of looking at it, then how can He be, as you say, a 'God of Love'?"

Her words in reply were courageous, triumphant: "*Experience* is not the test for the will of God; but *revelation* is. He has revealed Himself and His Will in His Book. If it shall mean to me an unrequited love for the rest of my life, still I shall abide by what He has said. I cannot believe He would say one thing in His word and another — contradictory — in my heart. I believe that for a Christian and a non-Christian to marry, no matter how much they think they love each other, is a direct violation of His Will. Such a union could never be commanded by Him, only permitted. He would never be able to bless it in the wonderful way He could were it otherwise. I would not lose His smile upon my life for all the human love in the world. No, James, though I loved until my heart were breaking, I . . ."

He read her face and in it his fate — "I should love *Him* more!"

When she had gone James wondered if he had urged her too much. Yet when he remembered the expression in her eyes which

assured him of her love in spite of her refusal to say "Yes" he
knew he had done only what his heart had impelled him to do.
Man has but the power to declare his love; woman must either
accept or reject. Even though she had said "no" he dared to
hope that the "no" was not final.

He admired the power of her will to remain true to her convictions, even though he could not believe her convictions were
right. In another he would have diagnosed her attitude as head-
strong. But with June! the word that came to him was "faith-
strong." "It is her unshakable faith which makes her the woman
she is," he told himself. In building the tower of her life she
had kept the foundation strong.

James was startled by a new truth — startled as well as
pleased: Instead of seeming fanatical, her philosophy of life appeared, suddenly, to be natural and right and *beautiful*. "Supernatural" she would say, "for its source is the unshakable Word,
the Holy Bible, God's revelation to man." Other religions were
man's unavailing search for a god who could not be found,
while Christianity was a *revelation*: God revealing himself in the
pages of His Book and in the Person of His Son. Thus God
was searching for man; man had lost his sense of God; it was
man himself who was lost.

All this June had endeavored to teach him in their talks together, and all this James did not believe.

He had arrived at his store earlier than usual this morning.
The mail had just this moment come. Glover knocked at his
closed door and handed him a large packet of letters.

"Thanks, Glover — by the way, come in for a few minutes."

Glover entered and accepted the proffered chair. He was
pleased at the invitation. Seldom had his employer granted him
this privilege.

"Tell me, Glover, how you happen to be a Christian, how you
retain your faith in days like these?"

Taken unawares, Glover needed a moment to collect his
thoughts. Only with June and Mary had he talked freely of the
things of faith. While this unexpected question from Fownley
pleased him, at the same it found him unprepared. In the presence of those who also believed, it was an easy matter to talk of

these things, but where the atmosphere was charged with skepticism, he suddenly discovered that his throat was dry and the words would not come. For a full moment he sat without replying, searching in vain for words to express what he believed. Knowing his employer's attitude toward the Bible, he feared lest this present interview should mean, in the end, the loss of his job as a clerk. He knew he could not answer without his reply being opposed to Fownley's views.

At length he found his voice. "I — I did have quite a struggle for a while. It was easy enough back in the old home church where I heard the Message every Sunday and where we had many young people who believed the same as I did. But when I got here and began to study the question of origins — well, the whole foundation began to shake. And when we took up Comparative Religions — it began to look as if our Faith was just another *religion,* just the evolution of man's idea of God or what a God ought to be. But that's all settled now. I don't have any more trouble along that line." Glover finished with conviction and a clear voice.

James had listened silently. How could anyone be so absolutely sure of himself?

"Tell me how it happened, Harwood."

Glover smiled, pleased that his employer had called him by his first name. His confidence grew and with it his courage. "Well, you see, I happened to get a lot of help from a book I read — *Mad World,* in fact. It said that evolution should be studied with the understanding that all its theories were just man-made, that none of them need be accepted as authoritative and disproving the truths of Christian faith — for there isn't any evidence that man has sprung from a lower order of animals."

Glover's tongue was fully loosened now and the words flowed freely. James listened, astonished at his apparent enthusiasm. Glover went on. "The book said this: 'Remember in all your study of origins, there is only one authentic account of the beginning and that is the Bible record. All others are man's mere hypotheses.' And it gave proofs of the mistakes in those hypotheses. Well, that settled me on that score."

"But the world's religions?" James asked. His tone did not betray that he might be interested for his own sake, only that he was curious.

"Well," Glover leaned forward in his chair. "I had already had so many doubts planted in my mind that I was almost ready to conclude that all religions had so much in common that they must *all* be good — if you believed in them — and that it really didn't matter much which one you accepted just so you were sincere.

"But I have changed on that score, too. You see, it's this way: Away back in the beginning after God had completed His work of Creation, including His crowning work, man, and after man's fall into sin, He, God, gave to the world the one and only method of approach to Himself: namely, by faith in His Son, who was to come into the world later to die as a substitute for man, who because of his son deserved to die himself. But *until* Jesus should come they were to offer animal sacrifices in order to keep the Saviour and His death for us in constant remembrance!"

"But the heathen religions of the world — all, or nearly all have sacrifices! They all have a story of a Garden of Eden and a story of a great flood and an ark!" James put in. "Doesn't that show you that your Bible account is also a myth?"

James had no sooner asked the question than he regretted it. For he should not care to prick the beautiful balloon of faith which was giving Glover so much enjoyment.

But the young man before him was not disturbed in the least. "That's the question that first upset me," he said, "but, you see, the very fact that these things are had in common by so many religions is evidence that in the *beginning* there *was* an actual Garden of Eden and later a real flood. The slight differences in the records show how the true story has become distorted. So —" Glover's face lit up as he finished. "That satisfies me completely; all these religions are but the distorted or degenerated forms of the original and God-revealed. Instead of the product of evolution, they are nothing more nor less — as the book says—than the product of *devolution.* You find that in the book of Romans, the first chapter, verses 18 to 23."

James had listened attentively, Glover's sincerity begetting respect. The conversation did not continue longer, for just then someone entered the store. There were many things to be done and they must keep busy. At noon when James paused in his room before going down to lunch, standing for a moment in front of the painting of the tower of Pisa, he almost fancied that it was a little nearer the perpendicular than it had been when he left for his store earlier in the day.

CHAPTER XV

The report of the kidnapping reached the ears of Mary's mother. At first she gave no credence to it, for had she not heard from Mary herself several times within the past few days? However, when newspaper men and detectives began to call at her home she became frightened and told them of the telegrams and of the letter.

Conflicting reports continued to come from various parts of the country that Mary and her abductor had been seen. June, believing that Mary had merely gone away with her husband, was not alarmed, although she was greatly puzzled. Mary's instructions, requesting her silence in the matter, kept her from doing what she felt she must do: seek the confidence of the police and, through what information she possessed, clear up the whole scandal. The one sentence in Mary's letter kept the seal upon her lips: "It would mean instant death for me should my whereabouts become known."

It was her love for Mary as well as her faith in her word which steadied June now. In her purse, neatly tucked away, was another letter. It had come to her, special delivery, early this morning. It had said,

"Dear Jun

"Don't believe all the scandal about my being kidnapped. My husband and I are happy and quite thrilled with all the excitement about me. After a while we'll tell the world. But at present, while they're still searching for us around Frisco we're hiding away up here in the hills east of Parmeda. Listen, June, do this for me — Come to Parmeda as quickly as you can, secretly, of course, and come out to see me. It's terribly important — all this publicity. My husband says it may mean another contract in the movies for me, so for a while we'll just let things happen. June dear, I want you to call at the postoffice General Delivery window here, and get

97

a package which Mother is sending. It has been there a day
or so, probably, and I haven't dared to call for it. Mother
addressed it to your name. When you get it, take it somewhere and open it and it will tell you where to find us."

The closing was brief. It contained an explanation about
Mary's having hurt her hand and being unable to use a pen,
even to sign her name.

An hour after receiving the letter June was aboard a train
bound for Parmeda. The wheels clicked off the miles as they
raced over the rails. June was keenly disappointed. She wondered if Mary's reference to a possible return to the screen
meant that she had forgotten her newly-found faith. It was
this thought that almost crushed her as she neared her destination. She had held her room at the Walhurst, saying she expected to be gone only a few days. She left no new address. All
mail and other communications were to be left in her room. She
did not tell anyone except the hotel management she was leaving.

Woman of faith that she was, she lifted her heart constantly
in a petition to her Heavenly Father for protection and especially that Mary might not lose her vision of Christ, that somehow she might be deterred from returning to the life of an
actress. She prayed, too, for Mary's husband. When thoughts
of her own trouble presented themselves she endeavored to
dismiss them. James was not a brother in Christ and, therefore, was forbidden to her. She must not allow herself to think
of him.

June did not know that Mary's mother had told the police about
the package. Nor did she know that when she stepped off the
train the man who followed not far behind was a detective who
would continue to follow her until she called at the postoffice.

Tense with the expectation of a new experience and deeply
concerned for the faith of her friend, June took a cab and drove
directly to the postoffice. She scarcely noticed the beauty of
this city of roses. Her one thought was to get to Mary as quickly
as possible. To June, just now, the most important thing in the
world was the saving of the soul of Mary. She had believed that
Mary was truly converted, but she knew that her return to the
old life would indicate that her profession of Christianity had
been *only* a profession.

She hurried up the steps to the big doors of the postoffice building, entered and approached the General Delivery window.

The man who faced her smiled affably. "You're next," he said, nodding to her.

Innocently she inquired, "Anything for June Darle?"

There was no tremor in her voice and her hand was steady. The friendly clerk disappeared to return a moment later with a neat little package addressed in the hand of Mrs. Silvers. June signed for it and thanked the clerk.

Turning, she bumped squarely into a brown-coated policeman who flashed his badge in her face.

"Just a minute, lady," he said, authoritatively, grasping her arm in a vise-like grip. "Are you sure you are Miss June Darle?"

"Why, certainly!" June exclaimed.

"That's all I want to know," he said, "I have been waiting to take you to your hotel. We've a nice room reserved for you, with patent lock and iron bars — come along."

June staggered and would have fallen but for his arm.

"No use to faint lady," the policeman said, "although we'll be glad to carry you if necessary. You're wanted for kidnapping! Come on — let's go down to see the chief first and have a look at your mail. Your room is waiting for you."

The police ambulance was also waiting and June was ushered into it, where, handcuffed and closely guarded by two officers, she rode to the jail. During the brief ride which seemed an eternity, she could only pray. She knew there was some mistake somewhere and that it would surely all come right in time. Like a flash from a dark and lowering sky came a brilliant ray of hope to strengthen her. It was that matchless verse of St. Paul, who in telling of his own prison experience, declared, "But I would that ye should understand, brethren, that the things which happen unto me have fallen out rather unto the furtherance of the gospel." How the words encouraged her and gave her fortitude! It was as if an angel direct from the empyrean above had been sent to comfort her. Suddenly June was glad and even in the midst of her fear — *unafraid*. She forgot even the officers on either side of her and her lips moved in that act of fellowship which, to her, was as natural as breathing. "May it also be *my* experience. May this thing which happens unto me, fall out also for the furtherance of Thy Gracious Gospel!"

Such a prayer coming from a yielded heart could never go unanswered.

Fownley, in his room at the Walhurst at six-thirty o'clock that evening was attracted by the sound of shouting newsboys outside the window: "Extra! Extra! Mary Silvers' Kidnapper Caught! Kidnapper! Extra!"

Hurrying down to the street he bought a paper and returned to his room. It was Saturday night and his store would be kept open. He would have time to scan the paper only briefly before hurrying to Glover's assistance. His reason for returning to his room was what he saw on the front page.

All day long he had been thinking of June. Concentration on other things seemed utterly impossible. The fact that she had not been in her place in the hotel dining room nor dropped in at his store as had been her custom now for some time, had puzzled him. When he had questioned Glover, that young man declared he knew nothing of her whereabouts. Glover's face had shown anxiety and his manner had disturbed James to no little degree. Self-consciousness had kept him from inquiring at the hotel desk.

A sinking sensation seized him and held him in his chair as his startled eyes read the — to him — horrifying news. June Darle was the kidnapper of Mary Silver! Caught in the act of receiving ransom money from the postoffice General Delivery window! Was now being held in the county jail at Parmeda! June Darle in jail!

In the confusion of conflicting emotions he read the whole news story from beginning to end. In glowing style the article told of the letters and telegrams received by Mary Silvers' mother; the communication with Parmeda and Berkeley authorities; the detective who followed her from her hotel in Berkeley until she called for the parcel at the postoffice; the $3,000 in bills which the parcel contained; and, finally, of June's arrest.

The article concluded: "Beautiful, nonchalant and religious, June Darle has been apprehended as one of the suspected accomplices in the most clever kidnapping of the past year. As yet

Mary Silvers, former actress, has not been found, but a confession from Miss Darle is expected tonight. Beyond the fact that Miss Darle has spent the past several months at the Walhurst hotel in Berkeley, little is known of her. She claims that her parents are missionaries in China and that she has been in America for several years. This statement is characteristic of the attitude she has adopted since her arrest. 'I am a Christian, in the King's business. I am perfectly willing to go to jail. I am convinced that my dear friend, Mary Silvers, will come to my rescue and clear up this mystery.'

"Parmeda officials hinted that the girl may be a religious enthusiast who needed money for the support of her missionary parents and took this way of procuring it. Search is being made for her accomplice, who may be hiding near the city."

Again James read the last paragraph, fierce resentment rising within him. To distrust June was impossible. Whatever might be the explanation of her appearance and her connection with the money, it would be sufficient. Had Mary's kidnapping been only a plot to get June into trouble? James suddenly rose from his chair, his face set and his whole body tense. He would stop this diabolic business. The only way to find out would be through Marlyn, who had seen June so intimately; who would willingly betray the girl whom Fownley loved.

At Marlyn's door he knocked, sharply. There was a stirring within and Marlyn's voice inquired, "Who is there?"

"James," he answered.

"Just a minute!"

The minute proved to be two minutes and James paced in front of her door in angry impatience. When Marlyn opened the door, however, he had changed his demeanor and was outwardly as calm as he could command himself.

"Oh James!" Marlyn exclaimed, her voice carrying its favorite silvery croon. "I knew you'd come! I've been so lonesome and — afraid! Oh, isn't it terrible — this!" She held out to him a copy of the "extra."

"I have seen it," he returned, displaying a copy of the same paper. "Yes, Marlyn," he said, grimly. "It's terrible! It's contemptible! The frame-up of some imp of Hell!" His voice suddenly shook with anger.

Wide-eyed, Marlyn fixed her gaze upon him. She adored men in violent moods. "What can we do about it?" she asked.

"What?" he demanded. "We can put a stop to it, Marlyn!" He fixed his eyes upon her. "I want to know what *you* have had to do with this!" He thrust the paper toward her, his whole personality concentrated on forcing her to admit the part she must have played.

"Me?" She drew back. "Why — I —"

All at once Marlyn was aware that she had actually conspired with Graig, although she had not guessed what Graig's plans were. She knew that Mary Silvers had been involved and that an effort was to have been made to obtain money from her mother. But that June was to have been made the scapegoat, she had not guessed. A wicked gleam of triumph flashed across her jealousy-clouded brain, the same thought which James had known would seize her. *This was June's just desert for having robbed her of James!* She finished her sentence: "I — I — it serves her right, the little hussy! She had it coming to her!"

"What!" James thundered.

Marlyn wilted. Realizing she had betrayed her feelings she bethought herself to assume the attitude of a wounded spirit.

"Oh, I — didn't mean that, Jimmy — I — you see — I —" She began to pout. "I've been terribly jealous. You've been going out with her — so much, and I — I couldn't stand it — I just forgot myself, for a minute!"

He did not move toward her as she had hoped he might. Suddenly he knew he must leave at once. In spite of the fact that he loathed her ways and her worldliness, he could not forget that only a few months previous he had thought he loved her — had told her so. Oh, he was sure now that he did not love her, as sure of that as he was that he *did* love June Darle. But the old memories! For the moment they held him, the power of her beauty staggered him.

Turning, he opened the door and fled.

CHAPTER XVI

At the store James found Glover as perturbed as himself. Only Glover's promise to June to remain silent kept him from speaking freely with James about what he knew of Mary Silvers. He did express himself in no uncertain terms as to his feelings in the matter:

"I tell you, Mr. Fownley, I am not red-haired for nothing! If ever I get my hands on the bird who kidnapped Mary Silvers, I'll absolutely lay him out. Boy, would I like to sock him right now!"

James' reply revealed his own mood. "Not only that, but he ought to be strung up for dragging a pure name through the filth of a kidnapping scandal!"

Glover, who also had read the paper, exclaimed vehemently, "And it'll give the skeptics and scoffers something else to spout off their mouths about!" He did not know that his bow, drawn at a venture, had sent an arrow direct to the heart of his employer. But James knew and later was glad for it.

At closing time, after an unusually busy evening, Frownley put on his hat and coat and with a final word to Glover about his duties early Monday morning, he shook hands with him solemnly, a thing he seldom did. "Good night, Glover," he said, almost affectionately. Their hands remained clasped for a moment while they looked into each other's eyes. Then James spoke again grimly, "I'm going to Parmeda, Harwood!" His face showed intense emotion. "No one needs to know where I am—I'm just out of the city, see!"

Glover read his eyes. Suddenly he understood the reason for his chief's deep feeling in the matter. Sympathy welled up within and he tightened his grip on the hand that held his so firmly. Unpremeditated, the words escaped his lips: *"And may her Christ go with you!"*

Afterwards Glover wondered if he had said the wrong thing, but he was not troubled, for he was beginning to see that to be a

103

faithful Christian involved being faithful to the promptings of the Spirit within. As he drew the window shades, preparatory to closing the store, he found himself saying the words over again, only they were now being addressed to a different Person: "Yes, go with him, O Christ, and show him what a Saviour you really are!"

Within the past few weeks Fownley had bought a new car, a high-powered coupe of popular make. Hurrying to his room he packed a few things into his traveling bag and made himself ready for the trip. "I may need this," he said to himself, as he touched the butt of his revolver. "But — no, I don't believe I'll take it." He thrust it into a drawer. As he turned to leave, his eyes circled the room, glimpsing fleetingly the painting of the tower of Pisa. "Still leaning!" was the thought that flashed through his mind. The swastika pattern on the rug seemed to say, "Good luck, Mr. Fownley!" But as he fixed his eyes upon it, the greeting appeared to be altogether too shallow. He needed something weightier, something deeper and stronger, like — well — like Glover's final words before they had parted at the store.

Twenty minutes later he was driving on the ferry at Richmond. The trip across the bay seemed endless. A heavy fog hung low and made it appear as if no progress were being made. At length they reached the other side. He gripped his steering wheel tightly as he followed the line of traffic down its narrow lane, off the ferry and into the streets. Through San Raphael he drove as rapidly as he dared, following with difficulty the right road. He had studied his map carefully, however, and little time was lost.

He realized he could be of no service to June at this hour of the night, but that didn't matter. He would, at least, be near her and tomorrow he would see what could be done.

From San Raphael he steered out into the broad, paved highway where one by one the little towns skimmed by. He drove desperately, not because there was any need for him to hurry but because he himself was desperate. Nearing the city he swung to the right into Parmeda Avenue and drove down into the heart of the city.

He would have driven around the city but he reasoned that police might be watching for out-of-town cars. He did not want to answer any questions tonight. What he desired now was to find a place of seclusion where he might lay plans for tomorrow. He selected a first class hotel, registered and went at once to his room.

How he managed to get through the night, he did not know nor care. He tossed restlessly on his pillow, catching a few hours of sleep after five o'clock.

In the morning he sat grimly in his room, more calm than he had been when he first arrived. Nothing new had happened during the night. June had not confessed and no trace had been found of Mary Silvers. He was keenly disappointed. The Sunday morning edition of the Parmeda paper, which he had been scanning, said that no visitors would be allowed to call at the jail on either friends or relatives. As it was expected that the girl's accomplice might make an attempt to free her, a heavy guard would be on duty at all times.

James scowled. It appeared there was nothing he could do. True, he might march boldly into the arms of the law and get himself locked up. This he feared would be the case if he began asking questions. He suddenly realized the futility of having come. There was nothing he could do, at least not yet. He must wait for some further development. So he made plans to stay — several days if necessary. While he meditated, church bells began to ring. She could not be going to church today. Once more he took up the paper. For some time now it had been his custom to accompany her to church on Sunday mornings.

He searched the church announcements, well knowing what type of service she would prefer to attend: "One where the true gospel is preached." He ran his eye down the list of notices. The sermon topics of several attracted his attention.

One read: Morning topic, "The Mystery of the Modern Mind." Evening sermon at 7:30 o'clock. Book Review: "Making a New Christ for a New Age."

Another announced for the morning sermon: "The Townsend Pension Plan," and for the evening sermon: "Jesus or Paul — Which?"

Other sermon topics were less startling, savoring less of icono-clasm, or what June would term, "Atheism under a religious flag." He decided that he might hear the true gospel in perhaps three churches in this city. At any rate he would, out of respect for her faith, select a church which she would attend eagerly. He noted the address and set out to find the church. He did not know that when his eye had fallen on that church notice, a winged prayer from the jail was about to be answered.

At eleven o'clock he was seated in the back row of a little stucco church. Nothing of affluence or formality pervaded the atmosphere. Looking about him, studying the faces of the con-gregation which comfortably filled the main auditorium, he de-cided that these people represented a fair cross-section of the residents of California. He judged, too, that simplicity would characterize the home life of most of those who were here.

In an attitude of respectful tolerance, in the midst of which was a growing sense of his own unworthiness, he settled himself to listen. He could not define his emotions. The unbelief of his past years seemed to have settled grimly upon the throne of his mind, where, like a tyrant, it beat down and drove back all the attacks of faith. He had decided since meeting June Darle that he *would* believe if he could, but that he couldn't.

He wondered if the tall, square-shouldered, scholarly-appear-ing minister who rose to speak could help him. Not that he ad-mitted for a moment that he needed help. Far from that. He had always believed that he was sufficient in himself — until the past weeks.

The service was short and beautifully reverent, the sermon similar in type to those Fownley had heard in Calvary Church at Berkeley: not a great, philosophical dissertation but a brief passage of Scripture unfolded in expository style and amply illustrated by current events of the day. James was neither bored nor disgusted as he had anticipated he might be. Rather, he was impressed — deeply so.

Afterward he remembered the one Scripture verse which had been repeated a number of times, *"I am the way, the truth, and the life: no man cometh unto the Father, but by me."* The clos-ing appeal left its mark also.

"Remember," the minister declared earnestly and forcefully, "that we are living in a wonderful age and if the Bible be true — which it most certainly is — we are living in the darkest hour of the world's history. Civilization's sins are fully as gross as those of heathendom. Not only is Christ the only way out for the world, socially and economically, but He is the only way *up*. No man can be saved or have any hope of heaven unless and until he has accepted Jesus Christ as his Personal Saviour. 'No man cometh to the Father but by *Me*.' He is the way and the *only* way."

The sermon was over. There had been logic, oratory, conviction. There had been something more, there had been *power!* Fownley was reluctant to leave. From every side he was greeted by friendly smiles and handshakes and invitations to return.

A jovial, heavy-set young man of about thirty-five years of age gripped his hand warmly. "Great sermon this morning."

"Yes, a great sermon — can't say I see it all, but I enjoyed it," James returned, warming to the friendliness and enthusiasm of the other.

Not for one moment had he forgotten June. How could he, when almost every word the pastor had said had made him think of her?

"Say, Mr. . . . ." the young man began.

"Fownley."

"Mr. Fownley; I'd like to have a talk with you. Rossage — Mel Rossage is my name. Can you come into the young people's room for a few minutes? Our Fisherman's group is going to the jail for a meeting this afternoon and we want to talk things over. Then if you can spare a minute more —"

"Surely," James agreed with sudden animation. It came to him that here might be his opportunity to at least gain entrance to the jail without his having to be asked any questions by the authorities. He decided that by all means he wanted to see and talk with June before he made any attempt to secure her release.

He followed his new acquaintance across the church to the side room, where a group of a dozen or so men and women were assembled. Mr. Rossage stepped immediately to the front and offered a brief, fervent prayer and addressed them:

"Fellow-fishermen, we have been accorded a high honor by the police authorities today in being allowed to conduct our meeting as usual. A heavy guard is on duty at all hours lest an attempt be made to free their new prisoner. She herself seems to be quiet enough, but the general public is pretty well excited over the kidnapping. There's little chance for mob violence as far as the girl is concerned, but if her alleged male accomplice is captured there'll be plenty of things going on around here. I pray that none of God's people will be guilty of participating in such a thing should it occur. Let us meet here at two o'clock for prayer before going to the jail."

James soon found himself alone with Mr. Rossage. "You say you didn't quite see eye to eye with our pastor?" the latter asked incredulously, yet in a sympathetic tone.

"Well — no, I didn't." James returned, seating himself at the other's request.

For a moment Mr. Rossage appraised him. "You mean you don't understand, or you don't accept his views — which?"

"Both."

"Oh, I see. Well — I think I know your trouble, Mr. Fownley. You've never been born again, have you? You are still — what the Bible calls — a natural man. I think —"

Just then the door to the room opened and an anxious voice said hurriedly, "Oh, there you are! There's a call for you — very important, Mel — come quickly!"

"All right, tell 'em I'm coming."

"My wife," he said to Fownley, as he arose. "I'm sorry, I'll have to go. You will come with us to the meeting this afternoon? You'll hear something worth while. We can continue our talk then."

Fownley rose with him and accompanied him to the door. "I believe I will, in fact I'd like to very much." His heart leaped with the anticipation.

His friend excused himself and hurried away. Fownley climbed into his car, drove to a nearby restaurant and at two o'clock was at the church again. He did not anticipate the prayer meeting, but curiosity as well as diplomacy encouraged him to attend.

Peculiar men, these, all of whom seem to be on such intimate terms with the One to Whom they prayed. They evidently had found something in life supremely worth living for. They all knelt when they prayed and talked to God in sincere, fervent pleadings, that He would direct them in the things they were to do and say. One of them even prayed for June, requesting that her incarceration might be used in some way for the glory of God.

When they arose to go, Mr. Rossage introduced James. "Mr. Fownley, men. He's interested in knowing what it's all about and I've invited him to come along."

"Good, Fownley!" several of them exclaimed, gripping his hand. "We're for you: it's the greatest thing in the world — knowing Jesus."

They arrived at the jail, a thousand misgivings whirling in James' brain. In spite of the almost irresistible pull which made him crave the thing that these men seemed to possess, he was beset with recurring — almost mad — desires to get away as quickly as possible. He had never met men of this caliber before. He did not know that the Fishermen's Club was an international organization with many thousands of members, whose one business was that of winning others to Christ, that thousands yearly were won by them and that they worked in harmony with the various churches of which they were members. Business men, students, laboring men, representing many walks of life, they lived for one common purpose — soul-winning.

Had James foreseen what experiences lay before him this afternoon, he might have yielded to his desires to flee the company of these men. But he did not know and his ignorance was bliss — for the duration of the meeting.

When they neared the jail and wended their way through the curious crowd to the very entrance where a heavily armed guard was stationed, the atmosphere became strangely tense as if some sinister thing were about to happen. James sensed that trouble was brewing and that he was facing a new and dangerous experience. His anger flamed within him as he thought of June behind those stone walls and iron bars, her pure white name besmirched with the filth of calumnious report. With his jaw set and his nerves tense he followed the men inside.

And so the service began.

CHAPTER XVII

In a lonely cabin in the hills near the city, a scene had been enacted the night before which was the direct cause for the startling thing that happened to James at the close of the jail meeting.

When James had registered at the hotel he had been watched by a man who an hour later reported his coming to Graig Warburne. A telephone call from Berkeley had warned of Fownley's possible appearance in Parmeda.

The road leading to the cabin was impassable at this time of the year and the place was so secluded that the nearest neighbor was at least a mile away.

"Well, Mary, how do you like things now? Are you about ready to do as I ask?"

Mary was silent. Her eyes, fixed upon her husband, were filled with loathing for him.

"Answer me!" he roared at her. The dim light from the lone candle on an old dresser flickered fitfully, casting weird shadows about the room.

"I have already answered, Graig," Mary returned steadily, "I shall never, *never* go back to the movies."

"Not if I can get a contract for you for a thousand a week?"

"Not for a thousand a day, or an hour or a minute — no, Graig, I'm not dealing with weeks now, nor with anything connected with time — but with *eternity*. Things have changed for me, I —"

"Shut up — I tell you, stop it! I won't stand it, do you hear me? I don't want any more of that religious nonsense!" He crossed the room to the dresser and took another drink from the bottle that stood there.

"Listen," he changed his voice. "I have news for you."

She listened from her seat on the dilapidated old couch to which she was bound. Except for a willow chair and the old dresser it was the sole article of furniture in the room.

His face registered malicious triumph. "I told you I'd ruin June Darle's reputation if you refused to do as I said — didn't I?"

"You couldn't!" Mary flamed at him. "Her name's as pure as the driven snow and always will be. She's the nearest to an angel —"

"I know," he interrupted, "she is but right now she's in danger, see? There are a hundred thousand men and women in this state who believe she is a low-down —"

"What!" Mary demanded.

"Yes, Mrs. Warburne, your beautiful, perfect little woman is in jail right now for kidnapping and for taking ransom money."

Mary stared while he laughed harshly. "See this?" He displayed a copy of an Oakland paper. Its flaming headline told of June's capture and that she was now being held in the county jail.

"I don't believe it!" Mary cried.

"There it is!" He thrust the paper at her and continued, his voice ironic, virulent. "She's in jail for kidnapping a certain Mary Silvers! Clever, eh? You see, your mother sent her three thousand dollars in a package to be called for at the General Delivery window in Parmeda. You had written your mother a letter asking for the money, see? Isn't that clever?"

"Oh, you contemptible brute!" Mary cried. "How could you?"

He ignored her words and poured himself another drink. Then he continued calmly, "And now, Mrs. Warburne, can you guess who is her accomplice? The man who has helped her in all this? You can't, can you? Well, I'll tell you that, too. There are a lot of things you don't know, Mary, but here's the truth: none other than our mutual friend and book store proprieter, Mr. James Fownley! Yes, and *he* is the man who may — if things go well — he's the chap who may have to suffer violence by the outworking of the law of mob psychology. Of course," he hinted invidiously, "there won't be enough furor created unless something happens to you."

He paused to watch the effect of his words upon her.

Mary knew her husband's temperament, had seen him do terrible things in years gone by, especially in drunken rages. Once she had thought him noble and good, her eyes blinded by his suave manners and handsome features, her impressionable nature deceived by his luring promises of a brilliant future. But now — Mary shuddered as she recalled her experiences of the past few days.

She felt his eyes upon her, and drew back. "You wouldn't — you wouldn't *dare!*" she cried, her voice choking with the thought that others — June, perhaps, and Mr. Fownley — might also have to suffer.

He did not speak further but disappeared into another room and returned immediately with a brown topcoat. "Recognize this? It's Fownley's coat. And this?" He drew from his vest pocket a ring whose set gave off brilliant sparkles. "You see these initials on the inside? 'J. F.' it says in old English engraving." He held it nearer the light. "And this —" He drew from his pocket a white envelope. "This beautiful letter was written to him a few days ago by — ah — Mary Silvers." He held it toward her and waved it so that she could see it. "Ashamed of your last name, weren't you?"

She recognized it at once.

"Here is the plan," he explained, "I place this letter in the pocket of this coat, see? — like this — then the ring with the 'J. F.' so beautifully engraved, I place in this little side pocket, carefully wrapped — no, that won't do, either. I just drop it on the floor so that it'll roll under your couch." He tossed the ring at her feet. "And then, just before I leave — are you following me carefully? Just before I leave these interesting clues for the police to find, I tie you up a little tighter and gently, mind you, at least as gently as possible, I place this chloroform mask over your face so you can rest easily while I am gone.

"You see," he continued, now talking more rapidly, his voice a bit thicker, "Fownley is already in town. The police will find you here and the news will spread like wild fire and the clues will point to Fownley.

"Well — you know what mob violence is! Fownley is registered right now in a downtown hotel. As soon as the crowd finds out, they'll all be suddenly transformed into a wild, hysterical mob. You see, you'll not only be chloroformed but badly bruised as well."

Graig paused to see if the threat would have its calculated effect. Then he finished, his voice savage, a fierce light in his eyes. "Oh, this'll be sweet revenge for me! On you, on June, on Fownley — the dirty, low-down —"

"Stop!" Mary was furious.

Seeing his threats fail, his temper and his liquor-inflamed hatred began to get complete control. He laughed harshly. "I'll *start* now with the business in hand." He glanced at his watch. "At 2:30 the police get the tip that you're here and that Fownley is in town. One hour later the news is broken to the town with a thousand interesting stories about how you have been choked and almost murdered." He paused. "How does it sound? Wouldn't you like to see your friend hanging from the limb of one of these oaks? And maybe his little sweetheart, June Darle, too, eh?"

Mary turned deathly pale. Graig moved toward her with the adhesive tape. Suddenly he seized her and with swift movements hastily put strip after strip across her mouth and around her jaw. "Your beautiful, kissable lips — I should have kissed them once more — all good husbands do, I believe, just before leaving."

Mary offered little resistance. There was no use. Instead she did the only thing she could do — pray. And she prayed desperately.

With horror-stricken eyes she watched him as he carried Fownley's coat into the other room. "Fownley leaves here in such a hurry that he forgets to take his coat," he explained.

"Now, my lady, I'm ready to put you to sleep. Let's hope they take good care of you." Stooping once more, he tested the cords that bound her to her couch.

Then he took from his pocket a white cloth and a bottle of chloroform. "This is next." Again he paused, setting the bottle down on the dresser.

She was breathing heavily. Having caught a severe cold from exposure the night before, she could only with the greatest difficulty breathe through her nose.

He lifted the candle and carried it toward her, watching the agony of her eyes, noticing her labored breathing. He hesitated.

"I'll have to take the tape off." He glanced at his watch. "Mary!" he said, in a more gentle tone, "I'll give you one more chance! Will you or will you not let me get that movie contract for you? I don't want to hurt you, Mary. Let's go back, and begin over. This is your last chance. You have just sixty seconds in which to decide!"

Sixty seconds!

Mary knew her husband meant what he said. He wanted money more than revenge but if he could not get the money, in his drunken rage and desire for revenge he might do what he had threatened.

A thousand impossibilities flashed through her brain, while as many frantic petitions for guidance flew heavenward — for immediate intervention of the Divine Hand. Yet with each fleeting second she seemed to feel that there was no use to pray, at least not for changed circumstances. It was expecting too much of her New Friend that He should answer immediately even when one was in the most awful danger. He, perhaps, might have a better plan.

She suddenly found herself praying a different prayer. "O Thou Over-ruler — not my will, but Thine be done. Answer only as the ultimate good may be for June and Mr. Fownley and for Thy cause."

"Time is up!" Graig moved toward her and removed the strips of tape that covered her lips. He seemed to do it almost gently. Even while his fingers worked he was talking. "I know you're not afraid of what I can do to you, but I warn you that there can be no mercy for your friends if you say 'No.' I've felt the pulse of the crowd and it is fast. Once let the mob get its hands on Fownley and —"

Her lips were free and she took a deep breath of the precious fresh air for which she had been struggling for the past ten minutes.

Graig looked almost tenderly at her. Then he turned away and took another drink. "What is your answer?" he demanded. "Your minute is up!"

Mary knew that to answer "yes" would be to lie, for she could not return to her old life. Already she felt the desire to use her personality in another calling, higher and more beautiful. "You still have your voice," she seemed to hear Mother Tilden saying softly. And somehow there came to her memory the dashing, laughing waters of Strawberry Creek as it came marching like a conqueror from under the University Stadium.

To say "no" would mean imminent danger to the life of the very one who had led her to make the Great Decision. Knowing, too, of June's love for Fownley, she could guess the terrible blow to her should anything happen to him.

She was between two harsh alternatives with a desire to choose neither. But her decision must be made. Lifting her eyes to him, she said in as gentle a tone as she could command:

"Graig, as truly as I live, I am not afraid of what you may do to me. *Here* is my answer! To return to the old life with all that it would mean in a denial of my Lord I cannot and I *will* not! I do not believe He will hold me responsible should anything happen to June Darle or to Mr. Fownley. But God will hold *you* responsible! 'Vengeance is Mine, saith the Lord, I will repay.' I tremble to think what may be the awful judgment upon you if your abominable scheme should be worked out. Hell itself would be too good for you."

His face went black with wrath. He had not meant to hurt Mary unnecessarily, but her last sentence snapped the cord that held his wrath in check. He was suddenly possessed with an impulse to *kill*. Thwarted, driven by the force of his drunken frenzy and his rage, he drew back and struck her. Again and again his arm rose and fell.

To Mary it seemed that each blow would crush the life from her body. Her only cry was a prayer, the substance of which she had already voiced. "O Thou mighty Over-ruler, make it all work out for the spread of Thy gospel — Thy Will — Thy Will — only Thy —"

Graig stopped for breath and dashed to the dresser for the chloroform.

But Mary was already unconscious.

There was a sound outside. It was only the crash of a falling limb as the wind played in the trees.

His wrath suddenly spent, Graig was seized with a great fear He was aghast at what he had done. Like a madman he stared about him wildly; and in his terror he dashed from the room into the darkness of the night.

CHAPTER XVIII

When the jail meeting began, Fownley felt strangely out of place. He was astonished at the zeal with which the Fishermen proclaimed their message. He intended, after the public meeting, when personal conferences were allowed with the various prisoners, to find his way to June's cell. A few moments' conversation with her, even if it must be in the presence of a guard, would mean worlds to him. He could tell by her attitude if she should want him to use his influence in her behalf. His very presence here would show her that he cared, that he still believed in her no matter what might be the opinion of others.

From the beginning the service was strangely appealing. Standing at the end of a row of cells, the Fishermen grouped together and sang a verse of one of the old hymns of the Church. A few faces could be seen pressed close to the bars. Otherwise, except for the guards, the audience was invisible. Fownley became keenly interested while listening to the first speaker.

Mr. Rossage spoke briefly, fervently. His opening words sounded the keynote of his whole address: "Friends," he began, "we have come to pay you a friendly visit today — not to preach *religion,* but to tell you how to get out of jail. I, too, was once behind bars, not iron bars like these. I was imprisoned, helplessly so, behind the walls of self-righteousness. I thought I was good enough without Christ. But what a fool I was! How thankful I am that He, looking down through the centuries and seeing my foolish philosophy of life did not pass by. He *knew* that I would not be good enough in spite of all my boasted goodness. For me, as well as for all other sinners He came to die, suffering in my stead and giving me His Own righteousness, which alone is acceptable to the Heavenly Father.

"I stayed away from church for years, almost breaking the heart of my Christian wife. I am a printer by trade and much of my work is at night, beginning at midnight; so I had a good excuse that Sunday night to remain at home. Unable to sleep, however, I turned on the radio. The dear Lord who loved me led me to turn the dial to a gospel sermon. I listened, at first disinterestedly, then more earnestly, and finally, with deep conviction striking at my heart. I was staggered by an overwhelming realization that I was lost and in desperate need of the Saviour.

"Hastily dressing, I hurried from my home to the church, arriving in time for the close of the service. There I almost ran down the aisle of the church to confess Christ. That night the Lord Jesus came into my heart. Things changed and I am now a new man in Him. The old bars of indifference and self-righteousness hold me no more. I am free in Christ."

Following Mr. Rossage's testimony there was more music followed by brief talks, every one fervent and convincing. The addresses were interspersed with a variety of musical numbers, both instrumental and vocal.

James became so interested that for a moment he forgot June. He wished that he, too, might be allowed to speak. With chagrin he reflected that there was nothing he could say that would help these men — nothing! He might tell them what a splendid example he himself was of the ideal man of today, honest and moral! But they would despise him for that, he knew. It dawned upon him that God's condemnation of his self-opinionated views would be even stronger than that of these men behind the bars.

The meeting drew to a close. One speaker, a Mr. Ferrand, a man of noble countenance and intelligence, introduced his message in a startling manner. More faces were seen at the front of the cells while he spoke.

"My friends, I am a mattress maker. I try to make the most comfortable, best constructed mattresses. Years ago I slept — both day and night — on the hard, lumpy mattress of sin. Perhaps my sins were not as contemptible as some but they were fully as hideous in the sight of God. I made my bed and I lay in it, just as many of you are doing today. Then I heard of Jesus, who said, 'Come unto me, all ye that labor and are heavy laden and I will give you *rest*.

The closing message was delivered by a Mr. Mannory, another of the city's prominent business men. One sentence stuck in James' memory: "I am constantly reminded of God's wonderful grace in taking my wrecked life and making of it something different, something more worthy of Him."

The last message was given, the final hymn sung, and the men separated to the various cells for personal conferences with those who might be interested. James, suddenly alert, realizing that the women's division was perhaps elsewhere in the jail, knew that now was the time for action.

"Where are the women?" he asked Mr. Rossage. "Do we visit their section today?"

"I think not. You might ask the warden."

With his heart doing somersaults, but staying outwardly calm, James approached the man indicated by Mr. Rossage. "Do we visit the women's division today?"

The warden surveyed him with apparent indifference. "There are only two of them here today and one is the Darle girl. No doubt they have heard the music and the messages. That ought to be enough for them today." He turned as if that ended the matter but James felt his piercing eyes upon him.

Suddenly the warden whirled toward him and startled him by saying abruptly, "I suppose you'd like to see her."

Astonished, James stammered, "Why — yes, certainly!"

"You know her, don't you?" the other asked shrewdly, his eyes narrowing.

Fownley steadied himself. "I most certainly would like to see her. She's an old friend and I'd appreciate a word with her."

The other laughed. "No doubt you would. Here — let me put these on you first." He produced a pair of handcuffs from the desk near which he had been standing. A strong pair of arms seized Fownley from behind.

"Pretty clever, Fownley — to get in so easily. Here, let's see how many guns you have on you."

Finding nothing they looked at him more closely. "You're James Fownley, aren't you?" the warden asked.

"I most certainly am, and proud of it," James declared, angered.

"And this is your ring?" The warden produced a gold ring set with a large sparkling diamond.

James stared at it incredulously.

"Is it yours?"

"It looks like one that was stolen from me some months ago in Oakland. Mine had the initials J. F. on the inside."

"You're sure?"

"Certainly!" James averred. "In old English letters."

"All right, sir, that's fine, we'll hold it for you in safe keeping."

"You'll what?" James asked, his anger still flaring dangerously. His astonishment, however, acted as an extinguisher to his temper and held him in check.

"Perhaps you recognize this also, Mr. Fownley." The warden displayed a letter in a white envelope.

Fownley did recognize it. Like a knife the memory of its contents thrust out to stab him. He seemed to see the gold-stamped title of the book, *De-throning God,* and to hear again June's accusing words, "But for my timely arrival and for the intervening providence of God, you should have been responsible for murder tonight."

"You are under arrest, Mr. Fownley, for the kidnapping and for the possible murder of Mary Silvers," the warden said grimly, his eyes suddenly hard. "This is your coat, too, I judge. You must be crazy to come here today in such assumed innocency and without disguise. But here you are! Shall we tell your lady friend you've come? Sorry we can't let you see her in person."

Fownley was stunned, his mind in a whirl, as they hurried him to an inner cell and locked the door upon him.

Ten minutes later Mr. Rossage appeared, accompanied by a guard. They looked at each other for a moment, neither of them speaking.

"This is a dastardly outrage!" Fownley fumed. "What kind of men are you to lead me into a trap like this?"

"I'm sorry, Mr. Fownley, I never dreamed you were Mary Silvers' kidnapper. Yes, I am doubly sorry. You wanted to know what it was all about. Well, I'm afraid it's going to be law instead of Grace. Fownley, you certainly looked innocent. I only hope and pray you will find the Lord Jesus Christ soon. You've heard enough of the gospel to know the way and —"

Rossage paused while his voice took on a softer, more sympathetic tone. "There's forgiveness even for murder, Fownley, if you'll only look to Calvary! I'm leaving this little New Testament and this book with you to help you pass the time — the warden gave me that privilege. May God bless you and save you."

CHAPTER XIX

The long, restless night had passed for June and she faced the new day, worn and tired, but still courageous. This new experience, so horrifying from the natural point of view, seemed rather an adventure in the great program of her life. Long ago she had discovered the happy secret of simply trusting when she was thrown unexpectedly into some new and hard experience. Having learned that matchless secret, she never allowed herself to forget it. Disappointments had been changed to "His appointments" and sorrows into sunshine.

Frightful — sometimes horrifying — things that would have driven an unfortified soul to despair, she used as building material for the house of peace in which she now dwelt.

Although she had not always been able to see her way out at once, still she had managed to cling to the Promises. Her cheerless cell looked out upon a dreary hallway to a row of empty cells on the other side. Unable to sleep on the hard mattress, beneath which there were no springs, she had resorted to prayer, not for an immediate and miraculous deliverance, but for those whose lives were to be touched by hers in this new experience. Again and again the words of St. Paul rang out their matchless, irresistible challenge to the tune of his prison chain ". . . *the things which happen unto me have fallen out rather unto the furtherance of the gospel.*" As the lonely hours crept by she repeated these words over and over, praying that this might also be the result of the things which were happening unto her.

The hour for church came and she was pleased that she was allowed to have a radio set of her own. She dialed at once to a familiar station and listened and worshipped, glad that bars did not a prison make. Out from the tangle of perplexing things that had come to pass in recent weeks, she sought to see the shining forth of the light of His promise. But as yet all was dark.

Things went blacker still when at two o'clock she heard the sound of shoutings on the outside and guessed that the spirit of the mob was being generated in the hearts of men. She wondered anxiously if anything serious could have happened to Mary, for which she might be held to blame. Then the warden came to her cell.

"Well, Miss Darle, the trail is hot. We've found the girl and things look bad for your accomplice. Miss Silvers has been found, bruised and suffering from pain and exposure. Yes, the trail is hot for Mr. Fownley!"

"Mr. Fownley!" June staggered mentally.

"Yes, ma'am." The warden's eyes were upon her, searching her face.

"Utterly impossible! The whole thing is a frame-up!" June affirmed warmly. Like a flash she recalled the scene in the Berkeley garden, Mary's disappearance and the letter received from her the same day in her own handwriting. She sought to allay her fears by refusing to believe what the warden said.

"Yes, Miss Darle, we expect to find Mr. Fownley any time now. His car is in town and he has registered at one of the hotels. We have his ring, his coat and a letter as clues. The Silvers girl is in the General Hospital, out of her head, suffering with a severe cold and fever and from brutal treatment. As I was saying, if the girl dies, it will be too bad for you and your pal. Things have happened before in this state!" He looked at her significantly, nodded his head slowly, his face sober. "And we have little or no power over the mob. The sooner you make your confession the better. Whenever you are ready let us know. In the meantime we're allowing you to listen in on the religious service here at three o'clock. You can hear it from where you are."

June was very much a human being and very much a woman. The tranquillity of her nature and her firm belief in God's overruling power did not make her a fatalist, bowing blindly to every fortune as do the Mohammedans, saying, "It is good, God wills it so." Her nascent love for Fownley had suddenly burst forth into the loveliness of a flower in full bloom. In vain she held before her mind's eye the perplexing events of the past twenty-four hours and tried to disentangle them, to see some semblance of harmony in them of the permissive purpose of the Guiding Hand. Without success she sought in the darkness for the tiny ray of light that would assure her of His care and love in allowing these things to happen.

Mary Silvers, suffering in the hospital and at the point of death! James Fownley, the man she — June — loved, according to the supposed evidence, her abductor! Of course he could not be. For had she not seen him in his own store after Mary's disappearance with her husband?

Ah, but of course the letter received from Mary had been written at the demand of her abductor! Probably she had been *compelled* to write it in order to save her own life! June's hands clenched tightly.

The hour for the Fishermen's meeting came and June, listening from her cell, revelled in the service, humming with them the hymns they sang. Oh, if James could only be present at a meeting like this. This was the gospel, not in theory or in books, but in the delight and charm of its outworking in the experiences of men!

The humming and shouting of the men outside grew louder and the atmosphere seemed to hang heavy with the rumblings of impending disaster. Oakland newspapers, on the trail of the kidnapper, searched the rooms of both June and Fownley. The negligence of Fallenby, who happened to be on duty when both of them had left the hotel, was responsible for their being unable to determine the exact hour when the two had gone. Detestives learned that two weeks ago Fownley had purchased a new car and that he and the Darle girl had gone away in it a number of times. In fact, there were those in Parmeda who insisted they had seen his car in the city more than a week ago. Some thought they had seen the Silvers girl in the car with him.

And so the rumors — tiny, harmless, dwarf-like when they first began — grew quickly to giant size. The citizenry of the state, still stirred to hectic excitement from the turmoil of the election, rode the crest of the wave into a state of wild frenzy.

In an Oakland gambling den, some hours after the close of the Fishermen's meeting, two men, the only two present at this hour, were engaged in serious conversation. Before them was a copy of an Oakland newspaper.

"Well, Blowers, it seems as if you've started something."

Blowers lifted his gaze from the paper and looked at his companion with startled eyes. "I confess it doesn't look good to me. Something's wrong somewhere!"

"You got your scandal all right, didn't you?"

"Plenty of it, but something's gone haywire!"

"Your friend outwitted you, evidently."

Blowers sat very quiet for a moment, his face a study in perplexity. "I tell you, Hank, I don't like it. And I'll tell you something else, too. I've been watching things and it looks like old Graig has been spoofing us. I've a notion he's one of the keenest birds ever. Look at this." He pointed to Fownley's picture and leaned forward, glancing about first to see if anyone were near enough to hear. A cough seized him and for a moment he was unable to speak. "That's the fellow who lost the ring in the park that night — the religious guy, you know, the one I told you about. And — listen — I've seen the girl, too, this Darle girl; and I tell you I don't believe she'd do anything like they claim. She's another religious one."

"That doesn't mean anything."

Blowers shrugged. "I'm telling you this girl is different. When they get religion like *she's* got it, they don't do no kidnappin'!"

"You seem to know her — maybe you're in on this, too. You'd better keep your lips sealed there, buddy."

Again Blowers frowned. His hand trembled a little as he reached out to take the newspaper from his companion. "We've got to do something about this and do it quick. I know it was Graig Warburne who carried Mary Silvers into that apartment."

Blower's companion was taking copious notes during the conversation.

Blowers continued. A wild expression was on his face when they rose to go. "I'm telling you, Hank, we've got to stop that mob or they'll break in and hang Fownley. God only knows what'll happen to the girl if they do. Can't you get your paper to run off an 'extra' to throw the public opinion the other way? To make the mob believe they've got the wrong man or something? At least until the Silvers girl comes to her senses and can talk?"

The man named Hank grinned. *"Can* I? Say, when the Herold screams this headline at the public it'll be *something!* Thanks, Blowers."

"You mean you'll really —"

"Sure! Why not? This is great dope, boy — great for me as well as for the paper."

"Here then, take this, it might help some." Blowers handed over a sealed envelope. "But keep still about where you got it, see?"

Pete Blowers, egotist and thrill-hunter, had had great delight during the first days of the kidnapping scandal, gloating with wide-eyed amazement at the sweep of the thing once it was in full swing, and once it was established that there had been an actual kidnapping. His hatred for Graig Warburne, for reasons that had accumulated during the months of their acquaintance, made him hope gleefully that the worst might happen to him.

But when it had become known that James Fownley and June Darle had been arrested in connection with the case, he became alarmed. Desperately so, when it appeared that there might be mob violence. He could not forget June's words to him that day when he had seen her and Marlyn at the bridge. He recalled with mingled emotions the glaring title of the book — as he remembered it — *Re-throning God,* which had stared at him so accusingly immediately after he had robbed Fownley.

It was the newspaper announcement of the finding of the ring that made him more sure than ever that Graig and not Fownley was the guilty man. When his companion had left he sighed with relief. He himself was safe. His reporter friend owed him too much money to try anything underhanded. His name would be kept secret, he felt sure. There were also other reasons why his friend would not dare to reveal the source of his information.

If the special edition of the paper only appeared in time and could be rushed to Parmeda quickly enough to get copies of it on the streets it might not yet be too late. Phone calls would do no good. What was needed was a glaring newspaper headline. An airplane could rush copies to the city in a few minutes.

CHAPTER XX

James, unaware of the imminency of danger, sat grimly in his cell, in one hand a green- and white-jacketed book, in the other, a small leather bound New Testament. He was still angry at the outrage which he considered had been perpetrated upon him.

Sitting on the edge of his hard bed, he glanced at the two books. Some inherent prejudice led him to toss the Bible aside. He recognized the other book as his best seller at the store. How many times it had been called to his attention! And how often he had resolved that at the next opportunity he would read it! Yet he had never actually settled himself to do it. Even now he fixed his eyes upon it with skepticism. It had been recommended too highly. He himself had recommended it to customers in his store, but his scant knowledge of it had been received from others and from advertising sent out by the publishers. He could not be sure that he wanted to read it now. In fact, he doubted very much if he should ever read it. Various quotations from it, which he had heard from the lips of others, were diametrically opposed to his philosophy of life.

He wondered if June had read the book. She had never mentioned it to him. He reflected on that for a moment. From all that he had heard and read about the book, it evidently was the type she would endorse most heartily and unreservedly. It occurred to him that her very silence might mean that she was anxious to have him read it, but that she feared to speak of it lest her enthusiasm prejudice him again it. Evidently the book had been written by some religious zealot.

He opened the book doubtfully, merely to skim its pages. He would never allow himself to be swept away by it. He knew what he believed and what he did not believe — at least he thought he did. He had no desire to change that philosophy of life. Yet, he admitted that this book no doubt contained the very

127

same kind of philosophy that had made June Darle the woman that she was. He knew also that something beautiful and wonderful—something extremely worth while — had characterized the message of the Fishermen whose service had just closed. Evidently they also believed in the book, for had not Mr. Rossage himself left it for him to read?

The chapter headings, as listed in the table of contents were interesting. Fownley ran his eye down the list. The first title caught his attention irresistibly. "Increasing Popularity of Suicide." The second aroused his interest as fully as did the first; it also angered him somewhat. The title was: "Heathenism in Modern Literature." That struck home. He scowled and glanced hastily at the titles of the remaining ten chapters:

"The Breakdown of the Christian Home"; "Moving Pictures and the Youthful Criminal"; "The Old Saloon Dresses up"; "What Price Cigarettes?"; "Evolution and the Survival of the Unfit"; "Communism in America"; "Churches in Name Only"; "Trends Toward Universal Insanity"; "Is Christ Coming Again?" and the final chapter, "What Will You Do with Jesus?"

"An imposing array of subjects," James muttered to himself. One could guess what the writer would say. Idly, he turned to the first page and began.

Merely curious at first he found himself reading avidly, carried along without effort on his part from page to page, from chapter to chapter. The minutes flew by, and by six o'clock he had completed the first nine chapters. Mingled emotions of resentment, keen interest, rebellion and whole-hearted approval gripped him alternately until finally he found himself in full sympathy with the writer, whose warmth and fervor and logic drew him on irresistibly. He did not wonder now that this book, although non-fiction, had quickly become a best seller. It deserved the widest possible circulation.

At this moment someone came with James' lunch and seeing him apparently deeply absorbed in the book, left him. Only a few words passed between them.

"Your friend sends word she has been praying for you all day, Fownley. You'll probably need to do some of it yourself before long."

Alone again James repeated the words to himself, "Praying for you all day." That meant she had been thinking of him all day.

"How like her," he said wonderingly, "not to think of herself and the disgrace brought upon her name, but of others." A lump came into his throat as he grasped the full meaning of it.

The lone light above his head was none too bright and he rose to his feet to lift the book nearer. The simple prison meal did not appeal to him and he left the tray untouched. He would finish the book. He was curious to know the meaning of the remaining chapters, especially of the last one.

He had scarcely resumed his reading when the same man returned for the tray.

"Not hungry, Fownley?"

"No!" Fownley answered shortly. "Say, when do I get out of this place? Haven't they found the kidnapper yet?"

"Sure, they've found him — he's here now — he came in this afternoon," the other returned, eyeing him significantly.

"Well, why in the name of common sense don't they let the girl out? Why don't they let *me* out?"

"Oh, you wouldn't want to get out now — not just yet. You'd better hope to stay in all night."

James did not notice the hint of danger in the man's tones. That there had been indeed some underhanded work which had resulted in his imprisonment, he was certain. But it never occurred to him that there might be mob violence. There had been cases of it in the state and in numerous places throughout the country during the past year, but to himself — the thought was preposterous!

"Glad to see you are reading that book," the man said, when he returned from a trip to another part of the jail. "Hope that last chapter wakes you up before you take your long sleep."

"Long sleep!" Fownley muttered. "What do you mean by that?" He endeavored to resume his reading but found himself unable to concentrate. This was Sunday night and the hour was approaching for church time. It was maddening to be so near the one he loved and yet be unable to speak with her.

The sound of music at his side drew his attention. He turned. It was coming from a pair of earphones hanging on the wall of his cell.

He sighed, laid aside the book and slipping to his bunk, adjusted the headgear and endeavored to relax.

A voice came clear and ringing: "Ladies and gentlemen, we now turn to the First Presbyterian Church of Hollywood, where you will listen to the evening service, including an address by the pastor, Dr. Stewart P. McLennan. His theme for tonight will be "The Darkness That Is Within Thee."

With the announcement of the subject, James gave attention in earnest, anticipating something along the same line of thought as he had just been reading. It was June herself who had once told him, "If ever you have an opportunity to hear Dr. McLennan of Hollywood it will be well worth your while. He is an outstanding Bible expositor. He will lead you to Christ if any man ever can."

Outside, the spirit of the mob was rising higher and higher in its intensity. A dull roar, as of a thousand demon-possessed voices shouting and yelling, reverberated, piercing its way through the walls of the prison and warning those within that violence was at the door.

June, hearing, shuddered in agony and fear, guessing that something terrible was about to happen. She was not afraid for herself; she could face the worst. Her all was upon the altar of her Lord and He would over-rule for her. Death was not to be feared by one who trusted in the blood of Calvary. To such a one it was but the door to the great beyond where "to die is gain."

But for James! He would be the one to suffer! It was no doubt he who was the target for the wrath of these men in whom the spirit of revenge had burst the bonds of reason, in whom all sense of right and wrong was temporarily drowned in the frenzy of their mad desire.

Pacing the floor of her narrow cell she prayed out of the agony of her heart, "O Father, O Christ, help — O God, I pray that he may be spared. Don't let him die — *unprepared!* He must not — he —"

There was a step outside her cell. "Don't be afraid. They're not after you. It's Fownley they want. The report is that the Silvers girl regained consciousness long enough to say a few things and that she is dying."

"What?" June demanded. "What did she say."

"Oh, nothing you don't know already. Her condition is the strongest testimony. All that was needed was her word that Fownley is the man who —"

"Oh, he isn't — he isn't, I know he isn't!" June cried. "He—"

"But the mob doesn't know that, and —" He paused. "It'll soon be too late to tell 'em. Sorry!" he added. "Now don't start any screaming or we'll have to put a muffler on you."

In Oakland telephone messages flashed back and forth. The huge presses of the Herald hummed and roared. "FOWNLEY NOT GUILTY. GRAIG WARBURNE SUSPECTED." The huge letters covered the first half of the front page. Several hundred copies of the paper were already being rushed by plane to Parmeda in a desperate effort to get them to the city in time to disperse the mob.

Mary in her hospital room had regained consciousness for a few moments and then in her semi-delirium she had murmured something about Fownley being innocent. "Don't let them hang him," she had said. Then she had drifted away again. It was this news which had been telephoned to the Oakland papers from the hospital. "Get hundreds of copies on the street here quickly! It's the only way to save the man's life. The governor has dispatched troops but they can't get here in time."

Warburne himself, having learned that the spirit of the mob was brewing against Mary's abductor and that it was generally believed that Fownley was the guilty man, grinned with triumph. His plan was working out beautifully. But when news came that Mary was showing signs of regaining consciousness, he became alarmed lest she tell the truth. He had counted on a lingering loyalty to him, but she might absolve Fownley and in her delirium she *might* also mention his own name! His anxiety grew suddenly into a great fear. What if the truth should become known and the mob in its blind frenzy turned to him! Why had he not fled from the city last night? What folly had led him to decide it was safer to stay here?

Shaking with emotion, driven by an awakened conscience, which seemed to shout at him his guilt, he became terrified. He had not really meant to go this far. *Suppose Mary should not recover!* That would mean that he had murdered her!

He dashed from his room and rushed into the street shouting to everyone he met and running wildly toward the jail. "Mary Silvers is dead. Mary Silvers is dead! Get Fownley! Rush the jail!"

The mob needed no more than just that. Many had been waiting for the final spark to set the smouldering fury into a wild flame of madness.

James, with earphones adjusted, was listening to the message from the Hollywood church.

Clear and authoritative, the words of the minister rang out their appeal. The message seemed directed straight to Fownley. Perhaps it was; for had not the minister prayed that very day that his listeners might be prepared, and had not June also prayed to the God who "works in a mysterious way His wonders to perform?" "Yes," the speaker said, "it is harder for God to save a so-called good man than it is for Him to save anyone else. The average moral man is an egotist, rejecting the Bible and its clear, cogent message of salvation through Christ alone. The merely good man, worshipping his own finite philosophy of life, rejecting the light of the old Book, walks vainly in the boasted light of his own intelligence. God's power is just the same in his case as in any other, but the man's proud clinging to his own righteousness keeps him beyond the pale of redemption. Our Lord Jesus speaks of men being cast out into outer darkness, and He means just that. *All* unsaved men who will not turn to Christ, no matter how moral or how civilized, *will* be cast out into outer darkness — into the long, dark night of a Christless eternity!

"But there is another night — dark and dreadful — the very earnest of that more terrible night to come. This is the night which unsaved men now have in their own hearts as they blindly grope along through life without God. It is the darkness within! Jesus said also, 'If the light that is in thee (meaning the light you merely think you have) be *darkness,* how great is that darkness?' My friends, there is a double darkness, a two-fold night — the night of *time* and the night of *eternity.*"

That was all that Fownley heard of the message. The mob had rushed upon the jail.

CHAPTER XXI

Mob! What a word to strike terror to the heart! A turbulent, lawless crowd of uncontrolled men, rich and poor alike! Uncontrolled? Nay, *controlled*. Not restrained, but governed and driven by the force of raging emotions. A thousand men with one thought predominant, their eyes dimmed to the finer things of life, one frenzied desire pressing hotly upon their minds!

Like the swine that rushed headlong into the sea in days of old, so tonight, driving blindly through they rushed headlong upon the jail. Clubs cracked the barrage of tear gas bombs and swinging clubs fell mercilessly upon bared heads! Still the mob rushed on, blind, furious, crazed, bent on one thing, — judgment upon the kidnapper-slayer of Mary Silvers!

In her hospital room Mary stirred restlessly upon her pillow. Dull, throbbing pain pounded at her temples. Faintly at first she recalled her experiences in the cabin. Her last memory was of Graig standing over her, with livid face, his breath coming hard, his arm flailing her with brutal blows.

But it was not memory of the pain or of the terrible beating which now haunted her. There was something else! Dimly, it hung on the horizon of her mind. What was it?

Her room was on the first and only floor of the hospital. The window on the north was open. She had been placed here so that she might be far away from the noise of the town. The shoutings of the mob could be heard only faintly. In the hall outside her door, nurses paused, talking in subdued tones. One sentence came to Mary's ears, "They'll hang him; he won't have a chance." Overhead an airplane roared as if flying very low.

"They'll hang him!" Mary caught the words and their meaning unfolded to her slowly awakening senses. She roused herself and sat up in bed, only to fall back, exhausted, upon her pillow. Again she caught the whispered words, "Fownley . . .

134

the mob." Then the footsteps faded away down the hall. Between her and the door was a thin hospital screen.

As her awakening brain regained its normalcy, a daring hope sprang up in her breast. Perhaps —

Her eyes fell on a small door on the far side of the room. Could it be? — had her clothes been placed there?

The shouting of the mob grew louder and Mary guessed the awful truth. Her hope sprang suddenly into a reckless resolve. If she could find her clothes! — she studied the open French window. Only a fragile screen to bar her from the world outside!

A faltering prayer for strength flew skyward to mingle in its heavenward flight with another of the same kind, flying desperately from June's prison cell. Together the two stormed the Throne above to cry in frantic pleading: "O, don't let him die unprepared . . . Use me to save his life . . . for Jesus' sake!"

"If any two of you shall be agreed on earth as touching anything that they shall ask, it shall be done for them of my Father which is in heaven." This promise, given long ago by the Lord Himself while He yet tabernacled among men — was it still available for those in need? Were the motives prompting the prayers of these two children of God unselfish? Could the answering of their prayers truly glorify the Father in the Son? Would the One whose lips had uttered this promise years ago deem that the conditions had been fully met and *would* He intervene? Or would He have a still better plan?

A rugged old oak, with low swinging branches, grew on a vacant lot near the hospital. It was to this that the mob was rushing its helpless victim. "Let him die outside her hospital room!" someone had shouted. And the cry had been heard and passed from lip to lip. "The old oak behind the hospital — hang him there!" another had shouted, and that, too, had found favor with the mob.

Spurred on by the knowledge that she must do something, that she alone could convince the maddened crowd that Fownley was not her abductor, energized by the strength that is born of high purpose, Mary staggered from her bed. Police, leading citizens, the hospital staff itself might shout the news that Fownley was innocent; but only *she* could *convince* them. Only she could save the life of the one whom June Darle loved.

She found her clothes, dressed hurriedly, stared one fleeting second at her haggard face in the mirror, opened the screen and walked through the low window.

Already the mob had passed the hospital. The lights from the street showed a motley crowd of grim-faced men and screaming, hysterical women. Could she ever push through? Each step was an effort which seemed to cost her every ounce of energy she possessed. Still she staggered on, caught in the rush of the throng, pushed and jostled, now this way, now that, but steadily forward.

"I am already too late," she sobbed, as she realized the utter impossibility of breaking her way through in time to stop the hanging. In a last desperate effort she cried out, "Stop, stop! He is not guilty! I am still alive! Save him! I am Mary Silvers!"

But her words were drowned in a bedlam of wild and raucous shoutings. Again she cried, "Oh, won't someone hear me? Save him! Save him! I am Mary Silvers. He is not guilty!"

Beside her, a man's voice shouted in reply, "All the angels in heaven couldn't save him now!"

Mary turned to him. The light from the street fell fully upon her face.

A curse of exclamation burst from the lips of the man. "Mary Silvers!" he shouted. "It *is* Mary Silvers!" Seizing her by the arm he began to elbow his way with her toward the tree. Other voices caught up the cry. From lip to lip it roared in frantic screamings and cursings only to be met with counter shouts of denial. "It's a lie! Don't believe it! Hang him!"

But the confusion gained time for them and the uproar that followed divided the mob. Strong men, seeing her face and believing her words, half carrying, half dragging her, pushed her forward toward the tree.

"Stop!" Mary cried, as they arrived at the tree itself. She felt suddenly very weak, as if she were going to faint. Wild hands were pulling at a rope, one end of which had been thrown over the limb of the tree. They would not be stopped. Shouting, swearing, their faces wild with fierce emotion, they pulled their blindfolded, struggling victim from the ground.

"Take off the mask! We want to see his face!" someone shouted.

A hand reached up, seized the blindfold and tore it off.

A scream of horror broke from Mary's lips as she glimpsed his face: "Graig!" she cried, "Graig!" Her strength gave way and she sank into unconsciousness.

Grim-visaged men seeing her faint, their minds still under the spell of the lust to kill, continued as they had begun. Ten minutes later a dishevelled, pitiful figure dangled limply from the limb of the tree above.

Its fury spent, the mob dispersed. Strong men of standing in the business world, women of refinement and culture, faced one another with grim countenances and turned silently to wend their ways homeward. Caught in the maelstrom — victims of the inexorable law of mob psychology — they had been tossed and swirled by its raging flood into the very vortex of uncontrolled passion. Murder in the name of justice! Crime, perpetrated by the hands of the few and approved and precipitated by thousands!

CHAPTER XXII

A week slipped by. Newspapers had already found a new thing to hold the attention of the public. America could not long remember a mere kidnapping or lynching. Other crimes of major importance and of more recent occurrence already claimed the attention of the state and nation.

But to a few within the inner circle, whose lives had felt the sting and the pain of the thing, its memories were not easily effaced.

The Reverend Mr. Warburne, pastor of Calvary Church in Berkeley, suffered perhaps the most. Being the nearest living relative of the lynched man, the tragedy cut deeply into his soul and for the moment he bowed under the weight of it. It was to him that Mary came for counsel and comfort. They met in his office. Mary sat in the same chair in which Graig had sat some months before. The minister's face was kind as he smiled upon her.

"I'm glad you've come to me," he said. "I was afraid — perhaps —" He hesitated.

"I know," Mary answered, "but after hearing you preach, I knew I could trust you. I should have come to you many weeks ago."

He listened quietly, sensing the battle that was going on within her heart.

"I've come to tell you," Mary began, "so you will understand more fully my attitude. I — I — Graig and I were married — had been married for years. It was kept secret. No one knows it now except June Darle."

The minister started. "Graig! Married!"

"Yes!"

There was silence. Then he spoke once more:

"Then you weren't kidnapped?"

"Yes, and no! We'd been separated. The kidnapping, so-called, was a scheme. You see, he wanted me to go back into the movies."

"But the money! He needed money, did he not?"

"I don't know — perhaps. For some reason he seemed to hate June and Mr. Fownley. He knew that it was because June showed me a better way that I would not go back to the old way of living, as he wanted me to. And I think he hated Fownley because both June and Marlyn —" she broke off in confusion.

The minister sighed. He was deeply affected by his nephew's shameful end.

"I don't know why I came to you, Dr. Warburne, except that I thought you ought to know."

"I'm glad you came, Mary. You did the right thing. I can only regret that you did not succeed in saving him. It was a noble effort you made. I don't see how you managed —"

"Oh, I didn't!" Mary broke in, eager to reveal the *truth*. "I thought it was Fownley I was trying to save."

"But it was the newspaper that saved him."

"Yes."

He nodded. "If you had known it was Graig —"

"I'd have tried to save him, too."

"In spite of —"

"Yes!"

"You loved him!"

Mary bit her lip. "He was my husband."

Again he nodded, his grave eyes upon her understandingly. For a long time they talked, Mary telling him her whole story. When she was leaving, he said quietly, "I think you are right, Mary. Your mother ought to know. Perhaps it is just as well the public does not hear it, but she has a right. Now that you've found the Light of the World the darkness of the past can be forgotten."

"Thank you!" Mary smiled. Her heart was warmed by his kindness.

"Just a moment," he said, as if an idea of some importance had occurred to him. "Could you wait a while before telling your mother? I've a reason for asking."

So it was that neither the mother nor the world came to learn the truth. The secret was buried deep in the memory of those who already knew.

In Fownley's office, another conference was being held. The door was shut and Glover was busy in the store.

"I've come to tell you good-bye, James," June was saying. They were both standing.

"Good-bye?"

"Yes, I'm going home with Mary; we're leaving on the midnight train."

He fixed his eyes upon her. "You are coming back?"

"I think not. I'll be making Denver my headquarters."

"You can't stand California? You don't like its citizens?"

"I love it," she said. "The sunshine, the great, rolling hills and mountains, the flowers, the beautiful homes and —"

"But its citizens?" His words carried a note of pain.

"Its citizens, too. People are alike the world over, sheep without a shepherd, victims of the times in which we live. The thing that happened last week could have been duplicated anywhere in this so-called civilized world."

"And why?"

"You know what I think."

"Yes, June, I do." He said the word June softly, reverently. He liked to say it that way. "But I want to hear you say it again before you go."

She saw that he meant it and she gave him the answer he expected: "They are without a shepherd because they do not have the Great Shepherd."

"Thank you," he said.

She turned to go, a wistful smile playing about her lips.

"You are really going? Is it good-bye?" His eyes were pleading, searching. He stepped nearer. "It has been beautiful to have known you, June. I've been made a better man, more happy and —" He did not finish the sentence.

"I am glad," she assured him, "I shall always be glad and shall always — remember."

Both their hands found the doorknob at the same time. It was only his respect for her that held him in check and enabled him to refrain from taking her in his arms. The thrill of the touch of her hand was sacred to him. Yet he felt that in her sight he had no claim even to that privilege.

"You will write — you will let *me* write?" he asked.

She did not answer at first. The battle in her heart was fully as great as that in his own. For a moment she waited, longing to answer him as she knew he would have her. But faith in the unchanging Word of God conquered: "Be ye not unequally yoked together with unbelievers."

The words came rushing to her rescue and their authority pressed upon her mind. She must not be swayed by the emotion of the moment. She must obey the command — if necessary — by the power of will alone. And with the resolve, came the strength to carry it out.

"Would it not be better — easier — if we did not write?"

His eyes revealed his misery and his lips moved as if to speak, but somehow the words were slow in coming. "I will respect your wish, June," he said. "Good-bye — and — and — God keep you always as true to Him as you are now, always a glowing testimony to His power and reality." He bowed his head. Then, lifting her hand he kissed it reverently, and, opening the door, he allowed her to go.

Alone in his office, he bowed his head and suffered. There was something more he had wanted to tell her, something he knew would have made her heart leap with joy, but he had not dared. Now that she was gone, he was glad that he had kept silent. It was better so.

A week slipped by during which time James struggled in the greatest battle in which he had as yet fought. Soul battles were new things to him and he was only beginning to learn that the secret of victory lay in yielding the whole conflict to the Conqueror of Calvary.

He was alone in his office when the crisis hour arrived. Reaching into a drawer in his desk, he drew out the little New Testament which had been given him at the jail. Carefully — almost caressingly — he turned the pages to a familiar passage, one that had claimed his attention often during the two days he had remained in the jail before Mary had been able to secure his and June's release. It was only the day following the lynching that he had learned that the fury of the mob had been first directed against him and that it was the arrival of the Oakland newspapers with their declaration of his innocence which had saved him. There had been a picture of Graig on the front page. Some one in the crowd had identified him and thus the terrible justice had been meted out.

"Come unto me, all ye that labor and are heavy laden, and I will give you rest. Take your yoke upon you and learn of Me; for I am meek and lowly in heart; and ye shall find rest unto your souls." This was what made June happy and satisfied. He turned to another passage: *"For God so loved the world that He gave His only begotten Son, that whosoever believeth on Him should not perish, but should have everlasting life."*

Long and earnestly Fownley read and re-read the passages of Scripture. Then he closed the book, placed it in his vest pocket. A strange new light was in his eyes and a fixity of purpose on his face. He rose and went out into the store.

Glover studied the face of his chief, knowing that he was passing through a great struggle. He, too, felt the pressure of loneliness, for a strong and beautiful love for Mary Silvers had sprung up in his own breast. No one had told him of her former marriage and he had only guessed that there had been a great sorrow in her life. Often he had thought of old Strawberry Creek and its triumphant emergence from its long, dark culvert under the Stadium.

The men faced each other a moment, amidst the silence of the book shelves. Strong men they were and kindred sympathies had drawn them close together.

James spoke first. "Do you remember, Glover, what you said to me that Saturday night before I left for Parmeda?"

Glover's eyes lit up with expectancy. "I most certainly do."

After another moment of silence, James spoke again. There was a new note in his voice which touched a responsive chord in Glover's soul: *"I — I found her Christ there, Harwood, and I have brought Him back with me!"*

A soft light shone in Glover's eyes and his hand reached out to clasp that of his employer in a vise-like grip.

"And now!" James said, "we will start our spring house cleaning. It may be out of season but it is not too late to begin."

Glover stared at his employer in amazement, watched him while he went to the display window and quickly removed one book after another. "These go first," Fownley said. He piled an armload of books on the little table near the first row of shelves. His jaw was set and the light of a firm resolution played on his features. "This and this and this and all of these — every sex book in the store; every work of atheism; every book that casts any aspersions on the Bible and its plain teachings; all of Paine's, Ingersoll's, Darwin's, McCabe's, Glyn's — everything —"

"What are you going to do?" Glover asked in astonishment.

"Do!" Fownley returned. "Can't you guess? This store is under new management!"

Glover stared at him in glad amazement. "You mean it?"

"I most certainly do!"

Glover let out a joyous exclamation of approval.

"Will you help me?" Fownley asked.

"Will I? Watch me!" Glover threw off his coat and started in.

Till long after closing time the men worked, their labor made more joyous by the knowledge that they were "working out" the salvation that had already been wrought within.

"Have you considered how much this may cost?" Glover asked. In his hand he held a copy of a work on sociology, entitled, *The Ethics of the New Morality,* by a popular American university professor. "We may lose some of our student trade."

"I am not afraid of how much it may cost, Harwood, I am only concerned now that I may truly show myself a new creature in Christ. If I lose customers I shall be sorry but at least I will not have lost my soul nor be responsible for the loss of others. That book goes out with the sex novel."

"Here's a copy of *Twentieth Century Use of the Bible*. What about that?"

Fownley looked at the name of the author. "That goes out, too. The author is a professing Christian, but the book is no more than religious atheism. It was that book which first started me on the road to skepticism."

Glover smiled. "You have the real thing all right, Mr. Fownley, yes, sir. Our pastor used to say that when a professing Christian can discern between Modernism and real Christianity, it is certain evidence he has been truly born again."

Happily, like two school boys playing a great game, they worked until past ten o'clock. When they finished, the store windows had a new display. In the center of one of them lay a large open Bible. Grouped around in an attractive arrangement were some of the latest Christian novels and theological books. The other window had a display of books of a clean and wholesome type. They left the lights on in the windows and closed the store. Outside they paused to look within at the new arrangement.

"You don't know how happy I am," Glover exclaimed, while they stood with their eyes fixed upon the open Bible. "It makes me feel like a slacker now when I think of how I worked for you all along without telling you how I felt about some of the things we were selling -- I guess I was too big a coward."

Fownley slipped his arm through that of his employee. "We'll forget the past, Harwood."

When they were about to leave, a stranger sauntered up and stood looking at the open Bible with the soft lights playing upon it. He did not seem to notice the two men. A mumbled sentence escaped his lips, "Hm! I knew that guy was religious all right." Then he coughed and sauntered on.

The two men parted for the night.

The first few days following the change of policy in his store were unusual days for Fownley: days of joy and gladness but fraught with continued struggles with himself. There were some misgivings as to the wisdom of the thing he had done. Would he be considered fanatic for discarding from his list the type of books which were now most popular with the majority of his customers? Would he be ridiculed? Could he stand the taunts of his friends? Did he not know of other book-store men, many of whom claimed to be Christians, who continued to sell not only the very type of book he was now discarding, but whose magazine stands featured the most daring cheap publications?

But each time when the struggle seemed about to sweep him from his foundation, he retired to his study to read again from the Bible. What would June think of him if she knew what he had done? Would she understand or would she believe he was merely professing conversion that some day he might win her for himself?

But temptations do not continually conquer the truly yielded man. He had felt the touch of an outside power and the strength of it was ever present. He had learned the art of secret prayer. Things that other Christians seemed to miss for years, he discovered in a short time because he walked, moment by moment, with God. Courage, too, came from the enthusiasm and approval of Glover. But there was another source of power of which he was to learn as the days went by.

Only a short time now till Christmas. Glover was away one morning, this being an exceptionally busy time for him at the University. Fownley had come to the store at the regular opening time.

He smiled to himself when he unlocked the door and entered. He wondered which of his customers would come in today to ask for a book or a magazine he was no longer selling.

No sooner had he deposited his coat and hat than his first customer arrived, a flashily dressed individual with a sickly grin and with marks of dissipation very noticeable on his face. He was smoking a cigarette.

"Yes, sir?" Fownley greeted him as he sailed up. "Anything I can do for you?"

The other looked about. "All alone, Mr. Fownley? I see you are. I want to ask you something."

"Yes, I'm the only one here just now — fire away with your question."

The newcomer shuffled nervously and took another whiff of his cigarette. His question was asked casually enough but it was startling to Fownley, nevertheless. "Say — ah — do you sell a book here by the name of *Re-Throning God?*"

The words instantly recalled to James his experience that night in the park and he was on his guard. He thought now, too, that he recognized the voice of his questioner.

"No, we don't," he answered, "we used to but we threw it out. It was not the type of book we like to carry."

"What? I thought you sold religious books here!"

"We do sell Christian books here. You are referring to the book, *De-throning God.*"

The other laughed, a hollow laugh that started him to coughing. He looked about the room nervously. "Blowers is my name, Mr. Fownley," he began somewhat hesitantly. "I reckon I might as well get straight at what I came in here for. You hear this cough of mine? Well, this cough means that I'm dying of tuberculosis, see? That's what the doctor told me yesterday. Been livin' too fast, he said, which I admit — but that ain't here nor there. I want to give you back your money and your watch. I lost your pocketbook or I'd give that back, too. I see you've already got your ring. I wouldn't like to croak with things like this on my conscience." He took out his own pocketbook, counted out some fifty dollars in bills and laid them on the counter. "And here's your watch as good as ever. I had pawned it to a friend of mine and went and got it back last night."

James watched in amazement, convinced that the youth before him was indeed his assailant of that midnight hour in the park. He wondered if the young man had also come to know Christ.

As naturally as breathing came the question from James' lips, "Why do you return these? Have you become a Christian?"

The other started. "Naw, I guess not, although I suppose I ought. I ain't good enough for that, but I want to get things off my chest."

"You're not afraid I'll turn you over to the police?"

The other eyed him restively. "If you knew I'd saved your life you wouldn't, would you?"

"Saved my life?"

"Yes, sir! If it hadn't been for me, they'd have hanged you instead of the guy they did hang. It was me that gave them old Warburne's picture for the newspaper. Yes, sir, *me*. I saw 'im when he carried the Silvers girl into his apartment and I heard her scream."

"I suppose you asked him for his picture right then, did you?" Fownley questioned, wondering how to judge the man before him.

"Not much I didn't — I just happened on to it one night in his apartment, when he was gone, you know. I tell you I felt pretty low when I thought maybe the mob would break into that jail and hang you or maybe that angel girl, June Darle, and I *had* to do something."

"I see," James returned, studying his visitor quietly, wondering if he were telling the truth. His thin features were pale and ghost-like and there was a feverish luster in his eyes. "Why do you tell me this?"

"I told you why: 'cause I want to get it off my chest." His cigarette had burned to a tiny stub and he looked about for an ash tray. James indicated one on the counter, while the young man reached for another cigarette.

"Have one?" he offered. "I smoke 'em for my health." Blowers laughed and held on to the counter while he coughed. "They help my nerves, too — keep 'em steady if I smoke enough of 'em."

"I see."

A great desire welled up within James to tell the young man of the new life he had found. Whether the youth was telling the truth he did not know, but the fact that he had returned the money and the watch indicated that some battle for decency was going on in his mind.

"Do you know June Darle?" Fownley asked suddenly. He wondered why Blowers had called her "angel girl."

"Naw, I don't know her, but I saw her once over in Frisco, and the way she talked and acted I knew she was one peach — honest and religious and all that. She almost scared me with the way her face looked when she talked about being 'converted.' That's another reason why I came in here today. I couldn't get away from what she said and when I knew she was a friend of yours I figured maybe I'd ought to come and talk to you —" He paused.

The desire to tell him of Christ came stronger than ever and in his, as yet, unskillful way, Fownley told him the story of the Cross.

Customers came and went but the young man tarried. He seemed eager to hear more.

"I've said my prayers every night for years," he admitted almost proudly, "but I haven't found any of the 'rest' you're talkin' about."

"It isn't saying prayers that saves," James explained, remembering something June had said. "It is definitely renouncing your sin and accepting Jesus Christ as your Saviour. That's the way you find peace! *'Believe on the Lord Jesus Christ and thou shalt be saved.'*"

When Blowers was about to leave, James called him back. "There is a way to fight tuberculosis with definite hope for recovery. I'd like to see you take the 'rest cure' as it is called — with prayer and faith along with it."

"Yeah, I know about that — the doctor told me — but I'd never stay in bed, *never,* I'm too nervous."

"Please come again," Fownley begged as he followed him to the door. "Let me be your friend."

"Yeah, I will — maybe. When you write to the girl, be sure to tell her that I remember what she said to me that day in Frisco."

"When you write!" James repeated to himself when he was alone. Bitterly, he reflected that he had promised her *not* to write. It would make it easier to forget, she had said. Forget? How could he? He chided himself that he had ever promised. Why had he given her up so easily? It came to him again that the one barrier which had separated them was now removed. In coming to know her Saviour he had become her brother — one in the faith — and now he had a right to pursue her, to seek with all his heart to win her.

And June Darle loved him! Of that he was sure! Was he?

In the despair and hope of the moment he endeavored to face the unyielding facts. He longed that she might know of his new life, of the joy that surged within him. Why had he not told her as soon as it had come to him? Why? He knew why. Because he must let her find it out for herself. Otherwise she might doubt his sincerity. *Then* if she loved him, she would come to him. There could be no other way. But he was not completely cast down, for in the midst of his conversation with Blowers there had been made known to him one of the most priceless truths of the Christian life: *the Holy Spirit reveals Himself in tangible manifestation in the emotional life of the one who seeks to win others to Christ!* He had believed on the Son of God and, having believed and confessed, he had been made an heir to the treasure that is far above rubies: *the Witness of the Spirit within.*

On this day when Fownley was alone in the store, there were other new and startling experiences. Completely given over to his Lord and utterly abandoned to His will and leading, he found no monotony in serving Him. It was like an adventure in an entirely new and wonderful world, in which at every turn in the road, new vistas of beauty opened before him.

He was finding joy even in the disapproval of his customers, not in the fact that his new policies were regarded with disfavor by them, but because of the gladness that came to him when he told them *why.* He found himself anticipating eagerly the arrival of each one, wondering if it would afford him another opportunity to witness of the One in whom he had experienced salvation. This was life indeed and true joy.

The aching void in his heart which told of an unrequited love — this alone kept the dark clouds hanging low. How would he have stood the test had he not come to know the Lord Jesus Christ in such an intimate way? His thoughts drifted to Marlyn and he wondered how Warburne's death had affected her.

The door opened and Marlyn herself came in. It was her first visit to the store since James had returned from Parmeda.

Ravishingly and gaily attired in an ensemble of transparent black velvet, she came mincing toward him.

For the moment he felt his old weakness return. He could not wholly erase from his memory the madness of his past love for her. He steadied himself, conscious of a subtle sealing of his lips, as if a restraining hand had closed upon them and a voice had whispered, "Now where is your bravado? Now talk about your Christ!" Her dainty perfume tantalized him and recalled experiences of the past. Again James thought of soft lights and sweet music.

"Glad to see me, James?" Marlyn cooed. "It's been dreadfully lonesome and you haven't called on me once — not once," she pouted.

"Anything I can do for you, Marlyn — any book you would like?" He braced himself and assumed the courteous attitude of a store clerk to a prospective buyer.

"Now, now, Jimmy," she chided caressingly. "Don't be distant. I didn't come in for a book; I came to see you. Don't you like my new gown?" Her red-painted finger nails glistened in the rays of the afternoon sun which poured in through the window. Her dimples deepened and she laid her hand upon his arm.

"I've quit smoking, Jimmy, and I've been going to church — all for you. There's the most *beautiful* church over on the Boulevard, with such a *wonderful* pastor. The music is simply exquisite and such fashionable people go there. Imagine *me* going to church! Well, I'm doing it and I really like it. It is so nice."

James stiffened and came back to normalcy with a sense as of coming out into the fresh air after being temporarily smothered in a smoke-laden room. Clearer than ever before he now understood why he did not love Marlyn. It was her utter lack of spiritual perception; she was devoid of any sense of appreciation of true worth. It was only her physical charm that had allured him. The woman herself was shallow, a gorgeous setting in which only a worthless, imitation gem struggled in vain to sparkle.

In this moment of revelation, Fownley felt a sorrow for the beautiful creature before him. She, too, needed his Christ, Who alone could supply the poise and charm which she now so painfully lacked.

A daring thought flashed into his mind accompanied by an exalted resolve: He would win Marlyn for Christ as June had won him!

His attitude toward her changed and for the first time since she had come in, he smiled.

When she left it was with the understanding that he would call for her Sunday evening, that together they would attend the vesper services of the church on the Boulevard.

Marlyn was so elated with her apparent success that she did not notice the changes in the display windows. With an air of affected queenliness she swept down the aisle of the store, blew a kiss at him as she paused at the door and disappeared without.

CHAPTER XXIII

The church on the Boulevard was "beautiful for situation," a magnificent structure of Gothic architecture, massive and coldly forbidding. When James and Marlyn entered they were greeted by liveried ushers who led them down soft-carpeted aisles to a favorable location near the front.

The organ was playing softly the strains of one of the new popular songs which James recognized as "When We Meet Again, Dear Heart." From the silent pews on either side he was conscious of curious eyes upon them. He wondered if it were Marlyn to whom they were giving their attention.

Appraising the service through illumined eyes, Fownley sensed the coldness and emptiness of it all. It was beautiful — yes — and formal, but — he shivered. In flowing, black robe, the minister appeared, disappeared and appeared again, followed by the robed choir. The voices of the singers were well trained. With astonishing agility they rendered difficult anthems and sang the responses with reverential solemnity.

Then came the address by the minister, the dashing, thunderous organ postlude and the services were over.

When James was opening the door of his car for Marlyn to enter, he remarked with dignity, "And now let's go to church somewhere."

"To church? Again?"

"I didn't say *again!*"

Marlyn was silent. "What do you mean?" she asked, finally.

"I mean," James averred emphatically, "that I wouldn't call that which we have just attended a 'church service!'"

"Why, Jimmy! I thought it was perfectly wonderful, I've never heard Dr. Feathergow when he seemed more grand. Didn't you just adore the way he gestured and the expression that came on his face when he talked about 'service'?"

"Oh, is he a doctor? Doctor of what?"

"I don't know what, but he has a D.D. and a Ph.D. after his name. Isn't it wonderful that such educated men enter the ministry?" Marlyn was serious.

James thought of his own experience and asked, almost abruptly, "Do you think he has ever been born again? Does he seem really to know the Lord Jesus Christ?"

"Born again!" Marlyn laughed. "Who ever heard of such a thing in our day? Who, besides June Darle and Dr. Warburne, believes in such antiquated teaching?"

"Who!" James' voice was vibrant. "I do, for one." He stepped on the starter and they slid out into the flow of the traffic. "Furthermore, I'm going to take you to a place where they preach Jesus Christ — not 'The Ethic of Social Progress.' Dr. Feathergow could say less in more words than any man I've ever heard. He made me think of a psychology professor, sitting on the feathery edge of nothing, entertaining at a soap bubble party."

He stepped his foot down harder on the accelerator. Marlyn gasped as they barely missed an approaching car.

"Where are we going, James? I thought perhaps we could attend a theater tonight. That's why they have the service at the vesper hour — so the members can have the evening free to do as they please."

"In other words, they are not doing as they please when they go to church?"

"Now, James, you're always saying things like that. Of course they are."

"I can't for the life of me see how anyone could enjoy such a meeting." James was serious, endeavoring to direct the conversation into territory where he could witness to Marlyn of the great joy and faith that was surely his and which he longed for her to experience for herself.

"Oh, well, let's not talk about it," Marlyn sighed and cuddled close to him as they drove along. "It's so good just to have you back again, to be alone with you." Her voice was crooning. "It's going to be just like it used to be, isn't it?" She slipped her arm through his, intimately. "Good old Jimmy! I knew you'd come back to me."

So this was what it meant to her! Well, he must not antagonize her now. He answered evasively, "You'll go with me to my church tonight? We'll dine in Oakland at the Jack-and-Jill first. O.K., Marlyn?" He assumed as companionable a tone as possible.

"You really mean you want me to?"

"Certainly."

At the Jack-and-Jill they sat alone in a secluded corner and talked, waiting to be served. James realized that he must not allow another moment to pass before telling her he had become a Christian. There was an immediate, impelling reason.

"Marlyn," he began. But the words struck in his throat. He swallowed and began again. Her eyes were upon him, flashing smiles and caresses. She was confident, oblivious to the conflict in his heart and of the fact that her whole worldly personality was arrayed against him.

"Marlyn, I've waited long enough, I —"

"I know it," she interrupted, coloring her prettiest. "You darling —"

He swallowed again and summoned his courage for still another attempt. Was the woman crazy? Couldn't she see he wasn't making love to her?

He came straight to the point. "I have accepted Jesus Christ as my Personal Saviour. I have become a Christian. I wanted to tell you before we ate because —" He paused again while she listened, seemingly amused.

He continued. "One of the first things I promised Him was that whenever and wherever I ate a meal, I would bow my head, either in verbal or silent thanksgiving. I thought you would want to know this so you would not be embarrassed tonight. I would like you to join with me."

A silvery laugh escaped her lips. "You do say the cutest things! The same old Jimmy, all over again. Really, to look at you, one would think you were serious."

James flushed. "I am!" he affirmed emphatically. "And I am going to do it tonight."

The waiter came and was no sooner gone than James looked across at Marlyn to tell her he was ready to pray. Then he bowed his head, conscious of a great inner joy and of the Father's approval of the thing he was now doing. Marlyn kept her eyes wide open. She *was* embarrassed, ashamed. What would others think of them! It did not occur to her that her embarrassment was being ashamed of Christ Himself.

The conversation was somewhat strained after that. It came to him that the unequal yoke, even in friendships, was especially hard for the Christian. At least there was no feeling whatsoever of spiritual fellowship in this hour with Marlyn. How different it had been one day last week when he and Glover had dined together in this same place.

When they were about to leave, a shadow fell across their table and a raspy voice inquired, "Say — ah — pardon me for interruptin', but could you tell me the address of that Darle girl? I want to write to her about something."

Fownley recognized his questioner as the one who had returned his watch and money a few days ago. Marlyn also recognized him.

"I'm sorry," James answered. "She has gone to Denver, I think, but that's all I know."

"Maybe *you* know." He directed his question to Marlyn. "Say, sure, you can tell me. You're the dame that was with her that day at the bridge."

"I am sure I can't help you," Marlyn answered coolly.

The other shrugged. "Well, if you find out, be sure to let me know. I'll be droppin' in to see you tomorrow, Mr. Fownley." With the utmost difficulty he restrained himself from coughing.

"Here." James handed him a card. "Look that over and it'll give us something to talk about tomorrow."

Blowers stared at it a moment. "All right — say, thanks, thanks a lot." He grinned gratefully and sauntered out, coughing as he went.

Marlyn's lip curled. "So you do know her address?"

"No," James answered with finality. "We'll have to be going now or we won't get seats."

The church to which James referred was the Bay Cities Tabernacle, an old garage converted into an attractive meeting place where thousands might gather. Here the Bay City Bible-believing churches were holding a united evangelistic campaign. More than twenty churches were sponsoring the movement. Their own services were closed on Sunday evenings during the three weeks in order to allow their members to attend the tabernacle. One of America's best known evangelists was the director in this Gospel Crusade, whose purpose was "that men and women might be saved."

The card which Fownley had handed to Blowers had carried an announcement of tonight's services. This, of course, Marlyn did not know, nor did James consider it necessary to tell her. His strength and courage fully restored after the victory over the prayer, he was thrilled with the prospect of the hour ahead and of its possibilities for Marlyn.

A choir of more than a hundred voices sang beautifully and enthusiastically under capable, informal leadership. An air of expectancy was prevalent and the message was gripping and pungent. The great crowd of eager listeners, the tremendous power of the sermon and the easy, yet reverent informality of the service were wonderfully appealing and impressive. Fownley rejoiced again and again as he found himself in perfect agreement with what was being done and said. At last the foundations had been strengthened and he was no longer "leaning." Straight he stood now, as straight as the Sather Memorial Campanile on the University campus!

"Ye must be born again," was the evangelist's theme.

A half hour after the close of the meeting, James and Marlyn returned to the hotel. He had not spoken to her of the sermon. She had been very quiet in the car. He wondered whether she had the capacity to appreciate the beauty and bigness of the message.

At her room, she said quietly, "I want to ask you something, James. Will you come in?"

He hesitated, then accepted her invitation.

Marlyn seemed troubled. "I may as well tell you now," she began, "that I didn't like the sermon. I think it's perfectly horrid — the things that minister said!" She was sitting very straight on the edge of the divan.

From his chair near the floor lamp he watched her, her hands folding and unfolding.

"For instance."

"For instance? Everything! I don't believe — I *won't* believe it!"

"Won't believe what?"

Marlyn's face was tense. James had never seen her like this before.

"That many good, moral people will never go to heaven!" she exclaimed. "That they have to be born again! I can't — I won't believe him!"

"Do you spell 'Him' with a capital letter? It was the Son of God Who first said that, wasn't it?"

Marlyn stared at him. She seemed actually to have a soul. For once, James reflected, her thoughts were elsewhere than on her pleasures.

"I don't care," she exclaimed, "I don't like to go to a church where I have to come home feeling like a sinner!"

"Well, aren't we? — aren't *you,* Marlyn? Do you think you, with all your worldliness, your dances and gambling, cigarette-smoking and self-centeredness — Do you think you could enjoy heaven where the Christ you now reject will be the chief center of attraction?"

Marlyn's temper flashed. James had never known it to do so before. In fact he had never guessed that she was capable of other emotions than those of pleasure and self-love.

"Are *you* such an angel? Don't I know you? Haven't I known you for a long time?" she flung at him.

"No, Marlyn," he put in firmly, "you *don't* know me. You know only the old me, the old, unbelieving, Christ-rejecting me. I am now — have been made — a new creature in Christ. 'Old things are passed away; behold all things are become new.' I don't mean that I am perfect, but I have a Perfect Saviour, Marlyn." His voice softened. "My tastes and ambitions in life are entirely different. I have a New Leader, a New Manager."

Her eyes were glued upon him, she read the sincerity of his face. Suddenly she burst into sobs and buried her face in her hands. "Oh, I *am* a sinner!" she cried. "I am just a worldly —" Her voice choked.

He looked on helplessly. What did one do when a soul actually realized his need of a Saviour and was seemingly repentant? What would a minister do? Was Marlyn truly seeing herself lost as he so recently had seen himself?

"Believe, Marlyn," he said gently, "believe on the Lord Jesus Christ as the Son of God. Believe that He came to save us from our sins, to forgive us, to suffer and die for us and to rise again and to cleanse us from all sin. Give yourself up wholly to Him, trust Him, live for Him. Trust not in yourself, but in Him."

She shook with sobs. "I can't, James — oh, I can't!"

"Why not?" he asked anxiously.

As suddenly as she had burst into tears, her attitude changed. "Give up my dancing? And all the other things? All my friends? I *can't.*"

A verse came to him. "What shall it profit a man if he shall gain the whole world and lose his own soul?" He quoted it to her.

She sat silent for a moment, finding in her tears temporary relief from conviction.

Fownley had never felt so helpless. He instantly resolved that at the first opportunity he would find out how to lead a soul to Christ, what to do and say in an emergency like this.

When he left it was with the developing realization that Marlyn had, perhaps for the first time, felt the convicting power of the Spirit of God upon her life, but that her love of the world had led her to reject God's offer of Grace and Pardon.

"Will you go again with me tomorrow night?" he asked as he said good-night.

Marlyn bit her lip. "Don't ask me that, James — please!"

When he had gone she tried to think. Warburne was indeed dead, which meant that he could no longer supply her with money. For years she had lived a butterfly life without concern as to how her food and pleasures were to be paid for. Whenever she had wanted money it had been provided in abundance. Her father's death had left her alone in the world as far as immediate relatives were concerned. Foolishly and extravagantly she had sowed the money he left her, until now there were only a few thousand dollars left. This, she realized, would go quickly, and then what? The longings in her heart were for a permanent and genuine love.

But with James a Christian, she doubted seriously if she could ever win him. She recalled her experiences of the evening and feared that with the new James she could never be happy. Either she must become a Christian or he must renounce his "fanaticism" and return to normal life.

The sermon had moved her deeply and she struggled to cast off its impressions, to stifle the strange emotions it had awakened. She thought of Graig, cursing his parents for having given him a tender conscience. Why did men have consciences anyhow? Why couldn't one go through life doing as he pleased, without constantly feeling a sense of restraint?

She finally arrived at a definite two-fold decision: She would never again go to hear that evangelist—or any other minister who preached that type of sermon; as soon as possible she would join the church on the Boulevard. In this way she could pacify the demands of her awakened spirit and could, perhaps, convince James that she was really trying to be a Christian. Later when his enthusiasm might wane, he would decide that, after all, being a church member was the equivalent of being a Christian. Of course, June Darle wouldn't think so, but then she was different. Her parents were missionaries and she had had childhood training that gave her a more Puritanical point of view.

Thus it came about that Marlyn set out to quench the Spirit of God, Who so graciously and lovingly had sought to lead her to repentance and faith in Christ.

"A dope-fiend religion," James called it when he learned what she was planning to do. It was the Tuesday following their visit to the tabernacle. "Instead of facing the fact of sin and unbelief, as everyone must do before he can be saved," he explained to her, "you endeavor to ease the pain of an aroused conscience by taking religious dope. It's not the stilling of your conscience you need, first of all, it is the operation to remove the cause! Oh, I wish you could see it; could see the beauty and satisfaction of knowing *Him,* the peace that comes from sins forgiven."

Her answer was far from the point. "If I did become 'born again' as you say, would it make you love me more? Would it make any difference in your attitude toward me?"

"What if it should?" he demanded. "You couldn't possibly become a Christian with such a motive!"

"Then you really would care? — a little more?" she pouted.

James shrugged. His voice changed and he spoke, almost harshly, "Marlyn, you're impossible! If you were half as concerned about what the Lord thinks of you, it would show some good judgment on your part." He turned to wait on a customer who had just entered.

CHAPTER XXIV

Time raced on, and with its passing James was endeavoring to forget June. It even occurred to him that it might be better to forget her entirely and to marry Marlyn. Had he not once asked Marlyn to marry him? Did he not even yet have the license in his possession? Was he fair to Marlyn in thus spurning her? Might he not win her for Christ?

Closer and closer he learned to walk with God, spending many precious moments in Bible study and prayer. How thankful he was that in his childhood days he had been taught many truths concerning the Word. That which he had known theoretically, came back to him now in experience. Glover proved to be a real brother and together they studied and prayed — and *grew.*

One day, a few weeks before Christmas, Glover asked casually, "What would you think of me if I should decide to become a minister?" They were in the store and he was standing with his back to the door when he asked the question.

At that moment the door opened and the one who entered answered his question.

"That would be fine, splendid, I am sure." It was the pastor of the church on the Boulevard who had spoken. Glover turned.

"Pardon me," the minister said. "I spoke involuntarily. Your question was not addressed to me."

Glover smiled. He had never before seen the man, but he had heard about him through James and others.

"Feathergow is my name — if I may introduce myself. Dr. Feathergow of the Boulevard Church." He smiled affably, and shook hands with both Glover and Fownley.

"Yes, I've heard you — speak." James started to say "preach" but felt the word should not be desecrated. Dr. Feathergow did not "preach," at least not the gospel. "Anything we may do for you? Any book we may show you?" James was deferential in spite of the fact that he considered the minister a false shepherd, a wolf in sheep's clothing.

Dr. Feathergow's manner indicated he was plainly aware of his greatness and of his ecclesiastical standing in the city. Yet there was something attractive about his personality. "I trust, gentlemen, I have not arrived at an inopportune time. I surmise you have been discussing things theological, judging from the question which was being asked when I came in. Young man," he directed his words to Glover, "I should be very glad to be of any assistance to you should you decide that your vocation is to be that of the ministry. However, since time is somewhat limited this morning — due to pressing duties among my parishioners — I will come directly to the purpose of my call — with your consent."

"Certainly," Fownley acquiesced.

"Thank you." Dr. Feathergow assumed a confidential, though noticeably condescending tone. "You see, Mr. Fownley, I have but recently learned of your interest in religious things, and that you have removed from your store those publications which are objectionable from the highest and most ethical point of view. I congratulate you, sir; that is commendable, I am sure."

Neither Fownley nor Glover felt it necessary to say anything in reply.

He continued, "I am not only pastor of the Boulevard Church, but I have been recently invited to deliver a series of addresses at the San Francisco Bay School of Religion. A most remarkable institution, by the way," he suggested to Glover. "My addresses are to be under the general heading, 'Christianity and the Modern Mind.' Rather a profound theme, I assure you, but timely and worthy of consideration. This series of lectures will be given to the students of the University also.

"Now, Mr. Fownley, I feel I can be of some assistance to you in affording you an opportunity to make known still further your interest in things religious.

"My lectures are being published in book form and will be offered for sale as soon as I have completed the series. Ah — I am sure you will be pleased to place the book on sale here. I shall have it anounced publicly and shall advertise it in the city newspapers. It is nearing the Christmas season and you should have a phenomenal sale, especially to the students of the Seminary and University."

Dr. Feathergow paused. He had said things of tremendous importance and had generously taken the manager of the Green Front Book Shop into his confidence.

He was taken aback by James' unexpected reply: "You will let us examine the manuscript, of course."

"Why — yes, of course — ahem — certainly!" That there should be any intimation that his book might not be acceptable, did not please him. Was it not a religious book? And written by Dr. Heironymous Feathergow, pastor of the Boulevard Church? A series of lectures to be delivered at the San Francisco Bay School of Religion?

"It's a religious work, Mr. Fownley, and fully in accord with modern thought. I am confident you will have many sales, especially during the Christmas season. The book is to come from the press in a few days, and I shall have a copy delivered to you at once. We are prepared to make you the customary retailer's discount, so that you will have a sizeable margin of profit."

Fownley gave a gesture of impatience. "I do not mean to seem rude or intolerant, Dr. Feathergow, but I believe I can give you our answer now . . . without examining the book. I'm afraid we cannot handle it. In fact I am sure we cannot."

The doctor looked at him, aghast.

"You see," Fownley explained, "I heard your address last Sunday afternoon!"

"You did?"

"Yes, and I am frank to state that I consider your teachings distinctly anti-Christian and a positive menace to the Cause of Jesus Christ. They are religious but they are not Christian."

Dr. Feathergow stiffened. "Please explain, sir. I consider myself insulted."

"No offense intended, I assure you, but since I have been saved I have accepted the plain, unequivocal statements of the Bible and all that it teaches concerning the Son of God. Your message Sunday afternoon savoured of the rankest skepticism and heathenism, the very philosophy which dominated my thinking for years until recently, when I experienced the new birth. Then things changed."

James felt a joyous emotion within and was glad. Again he had sensed the witness of the Spirit, commending and strengthening him and spurring him on. Filled with a great desire to give forth the truth that had made him free, he boldly yielded to the promptings of his heart and asked pointedly, "Dr. Feathergow, *have you ever been born again? Do you really know the Lord Jesus Christ?*"

"Sir?"

"I mean just that!" Fownley warmed to the subject, yet his voice was kind. "Judas Iscariot was once a preacher. I don't mean to insult you; I sympathize with you, deeply, for until recently, as I said, when I met the Lord Jesus Himself, I held your views. But I would have scorned to consider myself a Christian in those days."

"I have heard enough. I will not stand to be affronted further." The Reverend Heironymous Feathergow, pastor of the Boulevard Church, drew himself up with dignity and marched out of the store.

Glover and Fownley looked at each other in silence for a moment.

"Do you think I showed the Christian spirit, Harwood? Should I have been so unsparing?"

"I am sure you did just right. I admire you. I seem to remember the words of St. Paul, who once said something like this: 'If any man preach any other gospel than that which I have preached unto you, let him be accursed.' "

"But would Christ have treated him in any such fashion, I wonder?"

"Why not? Isn't he a blind leader of the blind? And won't he be responsible for sowing the seed of infidelity in the minds of thousands of students in the next week or two? Will not hundreds of young ministers go out to re-sow this blasphemous, heathenish philosophy in the churches of the land? I'm proud of you, Fownley! Such a man, to my mind, is Public Enemy Number One — The criminal kills only the body, but men of his caliber destroy souls!"

"That's true," Fownley agreed soberly. "Yet a man of his braggadocio type is not as dangerous as the more humble minister, who seems to display the more gentle spirit of Christ, yet who denies His absolute Deity, and is more subtle in his work of destroying the Bible."

Before they left the store that night, Glover said quietly, with a ring of determination in his voice, "I'm especially thankful for what happened this afternoon; it has led me to see my duty more clearly than ever — I am now absolutely sure I have been called to preach the Gospel of the Lord Jesus Christ."

After a few moments of silence, James said soberly, "I am about to decide something myself, Glover." In his voice, too, there was unmistakable conviction. "When Dr. Feathergow's book is off the press, I am going to find some leading thinker in the Scriptures and in the scientific world — anyway, someone who knows how to write — who will answer him. I may even decide to go into the publishing business in connection with the store."

The two men faced each other in reverent, determined silence, while their hands met in strong, steady clasp.

"And may her Christ go with you!" Glover's words of that other night, when he was about to depart for Parmeda, came to James in tender memory to turn his thoughts to June and to his unquenchable love for her.

CHAPTER XXV

The Christmas season came and went. Yet there was no word from June. Fownley continued going out with Marlyn, but each time he was more certain than ever that he did not love her. His love for June seemed to grow greater each day while the gnawing in his heart reminded him again and again of her lovely face and of the still more wonderful beauty of her soul. As a Christian, he had a right to pursue and to endeavor to win her, but he was bound by his promise to her never to write. Never again must he take the initiative. Of this he was certain.

In his despair the conviction came again that since he had once pledged himself to Marlyn, even though she had later spurned him for Graig, it was his duty to keep his promise to marry her.

He was alone in his room when he finally made up his mind. The floor lamp cast a mellow, green glow over the room. The green swastika pattern of the rug on the floor stared up at him in mockery as its symbolic meaning recurred to his memory.

"Good luck, Fownley!" it jeered.

He had been missing the fellowship of Glover considerably. Glover had not returned after the Christmas vacation because of the death of his father. He was needed at home and for the present could not continue his schooling.

"Good luck!" For a half hour James wrestled with his problem. Even the reading of the Word did not seem to satisfy; he was lonely and his heart cried out for the one he loved more than life itself.

June! June! It seemed he could not live without her.

Another cause for his distress was the fact that Dr. Feathergow's new book had proved exceedingly popular. Like wild fire it was sweeping through theological circles, creating wide-spread concern among those who cherished and clung to historic Chris-

166

tianity. Militant Fundamentalist leaders denounced it everywhere but in spite of that fact it grew in popularity. The spirit
of the age seemed to have prepared the nation for its icono-
clastic message.

James was nonplussed. He had not considered that Dr.
Feathergow was capable of such a work. True, almost any
scholar might have successfully answered him, but it was not
a mere answer that was needed. Already several scientific
books and brochures — both scholarly and well written — had
appeared, whose arguments easily refuted those of Dr. Feathergow, but none of them was able to stop the onrush of its
influence.

There was a knock at Fownley's door. It was Grant Weston.

"Can't stop now," that gentleman exclaimed, short of breath,
"but there's considerable excitement in the city! Have you
heard about the ten thousand ton caisson for the south pier of
the new Bay bridge? The one that cost three hundred fifty
thousand dollars to build?"

"No. What about it?"

"You knew it was discarded when ground swells through
the Gate seemed about to dash it against parts of the bridge that
were already finished?"

"Yes, I knew that."

"Well, it's got four men on board and twelve cases of dynamite and it's on a rampage, rearing and plunging wildly five
miles out in the Pacific — menacing ships and scaring everybody
half to death! It broke away from one of the two tugs that were
towing it out to Farallon Islands, where they were going to dynamite and sink it."

Fownley's face lit up. He jumped to his feet and cried out,
"Great! I've got it! At last, at last!"

Grant stared. "Got what?"

"Why, man, that — that's exactly what's wrong with Dr.
Feathergow's book. Don't you see it? That bridge has to have
two ends — one on the Marin County side of the Bay and one
at Frisco. So also the bridge to Heaven has to have the *Humanity* of Christ at one end and *His Deity* at the other. The Marin

County approach represents his Humanity and the Frisco approach His Deity.

"But Dr. Feathergow denies His Deity; and his book, like that caisson, is dangerous! It's not safe to try to cross a bridge which has only one end, see? The false teaching of his book is threatening to break down the whole bridge! It's full of dynamite and ought to be sunk. The only safe caisson on which to erect the bridge of Salvation is the Bible, the Word of God, which teaches the *whole truth* concerning Christ. Feathergow's book is a 'jinx'."

"You do a lot of worrying about that book, Fownley."

"No, I'm not *worrying,* but I tell you somebody's got to sink it! Or it'll menace every ship that tries to come in at the Golden Gate — to use another metaphor."

"I get you, Fownley. I must be going now. At any rate I hope they get that caisson in tow and blown up before long."

Alone once more, James leafed through his Bible. His eye alighted on a passage he had never before noticed. It seemed to leap from the page in flaming letters. "Here is the answer to Feathergow." The words seemed to say, "Believe and trust!"

Awed and humbled James read the verse, while its meaning found its way into a prepared place in his soul: *"For other foundation can no man lay than that is laid, which is Jesus Christ."*

In a moment James' fear was gone. God was still on the throne and He would never fail. The Gospel of Christ would be standing long after Dr. Feathergow had been dead and forgotten.

Rising from his chair, James snapped on the ceiling light and stepped to the mirror. "Thank you, O Christ," he murmured, "for the marvelous truth which has just been revealed to me!"

His eyes caught the outline of the painting of the Leaning Tower on the opposite wall. A grin of triumph spread over his tired face. He turned and crossed the room to study the painting still further.

"Standing!" he muttered, while his voice shook with glad emotion.

But he was still *leaning* toward June Darle! Ah, he must show himself the man she believed him to be — he must not grieve his heart away for a lost love. A resolve moved him to action. He would do the fair thing by Marlyn. Even though he did not love her, could he not learn to do so? Yes, and perhaps he could help her! He would sacrifice his own happiness in order to make her happy. He would go to Marlyn tonight and tell her!

Carefully he shaved and dressed himself in the suit she liked best. Yet, somehow, his heart was heavy as he approached the door to her room.

He hesitated before knocking. Should he? Yes, he had waited long enough. He must do it now. He retraced his steps to his own room. He would get the marriage license, which he had kept all these months, and they would be married tonight!

CHAPTER XXVI

Married tonight! Such was James' determination and it was with such a motive that he returned to his room for the license.

Again about to leave his room, he was called back by a mad ringing of his telephone. The night nurse from the Oak View Sanatorium was calling. "Mr. Fownley? — Mr. James Fownley? Are you the Mr. Fownley of the Green Front Book Shop? Can you come at once? One of our patients is dying and keeps calling for you. You'll have to hurry!"

James hung up the receiver. "Blowers!" he exclaimed, under his breath. "Poor old Blowers, he waited too long before going to bed and before beginning to observe the laws of health!"

In the hall, he bumped squarely into Marlyn, who had just come from her room. "Quick! Marlyn, go along with me!"

Marlyn was dressed for the street as if she had been expecting him to call for her. "Where to, in all the rush?" she queried, as they sped down the boulevard in his car.

"To Oak View Sanatorium. There's a man out there who is dying and wants to see me."

"Oh!" Marlyn gasped.

She looked across at him, but his grim, silent features told her nothing except that he was desperately in earnest about something.

And James Fownley *was* in earnest. He was being called to one of the greatest tasks to which a man can ever be called — to help a dying man see the Way of The Cross, the only way to be saved.

In fifteen minutes they were at the sanatorium. "He seemed to want only you," the nurse explained. "I suggested a minister, but he said, 'No, I want Mr. Fownley.' So I thought best to call you."

James soon found himself alone with his patient. The door behind him was closed. A lone, green-shaded lamp burned above the patient's bed. The air was cool and fresh from the open window on the east. On the pillow lay Blowers, thin and pale, his breathing short and difficult, a mere skeleton of the Blowers James had first known. He seemed oblivious to Fownley's presence.

Was it too late?

Suddenly Blowers opened his eyes and fixed them upon Fownley. "Thank God, Mr. Fownley! You've come! I —" His voice failed. "I — think I know the Way — but I can't seem — I've been such a sinner, Fownley. I want you to tell me again — to read to me about *the Blood — cleansing from sin.*"

If ever James was thankful in his heart, it was now. In this crisis hour in which all Heaven and Hell were concerned, he was to be used of God to lead this soul to Christ. Humbled because of the tremendous responsibility, conscious also of his own unworthiness, he opened the Bible and read. The truth of the death of Christ for sinners burned its way into his own soul also and confirmed him in his faith. *"Come now, and let us reason together, saith the Lord: Though your sins be as scarlet, they shall be as white as snow: though they be red like crimson, they shall be as wool."* . . . *"The Blood of Jesus Christ, God's Son, cleanseth us from all sin."* . . . *"God hath laid on Him the iniquities of us all."*

"Oh, I see it!" Blowers whispered. "It's the same as you told me that day in the store. I had to be born again; I had to receive Jesus Christ into my own heart. And I did it. But I couldn't seem to — be — sure about the Blood taking away *all* my sin — Can you — can you pray for me?"

"Yes, Blowers."

In the silence, while the stars peeped in through the open window, James bowed his head and prayed.

Marlyn, curious, had left the office and was walking quietly down the hall. She arrived at the door in time to hear the prayer. She paused, wondering, while strange emotions surged within her proud and worldly heart. As if glued to the spot, she continued where she was, not meaning to eavesdrop, but impelled by something within that would not let her go.

"Thank you, Mr. Fownley. The Doctor told me the truth. My — last hemorrhage — was too much — I should — have gone to bed — sooner, I —"

The exertion of speaking was too much for Blowers, yet he continued:

"Yes," he mumbled as if to himself, "All sin . . . the Blood cleanseth . . . It's all right . . . June Darle . . . she made me think . . . she . . ." The voice trailed away.

James sat silently, tensely, watching.

Then, as if something had awakened memories within the dying man, he roused himself and again opened his eyes. "You — love her, don't you? Why hasn't she come back? Why . . . ? She told me about Jesus first. She — she ought to know I have accepted her Christ, that I have been saved. I — there's one more thing, Mr. Fownley. I — almost — forgot. You — write her for me and — tell her that I — am not afraid — to die!"

James was silent.

"Quick! — Promise me — I want her to know. She told me — about Jesus first."

Still James was silent. How could he? Yet, somehow he knew that he must; he could not refuse a dying man.

"I promise, Blowers," he breathed, his voice scarcely audible, even to himself. But Blowers heard and thereafter seemed to lapse into a coma.

For a few moments James tarried, then rising quietly, he opened the door and went out.

The nurse was just coming down the hall. "He is satisfied," James said to her as they paused a moment in conversation.

"I am glad," she answered softly. "I, too, am a believer, and it is such a pity when they have to go out — unprepared, when the way is so plain." Tears came to her eyes.

"And He, Himself, is the Way," James said reverently.

"Yes," the nurse answered, "and a Glorious Way!" She smiled and the light of peace was in her eyes. It was the same light that James had seen and learned to know and love in the eyes of June Darle.

In the car once more Fownley was conscious of the presence of Omnipotence at his side. Marlyn was quiet, blissfully blind to the tremendous issues involved. To her, the realities of the life beyond this were vague and intangible.

"You prayed such a beautiful prayer," she sighed. "Where did you learn it? We don't have any prayers like that in our prayer book."

He did not reply; his thoughts would not permit him to. She went on, more seriously, "Our church has adopted the new Y.M.C.A. prayer book, you know. Such beautiful prayers: all about the new social order and doing away with racial prejudices and things like that."

"Nothing about man being a lost sinner and needing a Saviour Who can really save and satisfy? Nothing about the Precious Blood of Christ cleansing from sin?"

"Oh no, at least, I don't think so; but it's very modern. Dr. Feathergow said it was a forward step in religion, an 'emergence,' he said, 'from the cocoon of a decadent theological age,' or something like that!"

"Oh," James grunted. "And you swallowed all that!"

"There you go — making fun of our church again!"

James sighed inwardly, and chided himself when he was reminded of the verse of Scripture which began: "Cast not your pearls . . ." Another verse which he had recently memorized seemed more appropriate: "If our gospel be hid, it is hid to them that are lost."

It was nearing the midnight hour. The resolve earlier in the evening to marry Marlyn had been replaced by a desire to have a frank discussion with her and once for all to tell her that their marriage was an utter impossibility.

He drove to a secluded place far up the canyon-road, near the site of the C C C activities. There he parked his car. Not far away the waters of Strawberry Creek rippled gaily over the stones as it pursued its downward course toward the University Campus. Here, on other occasions, he had come with June and they had talked quietly of the deeper things of life, of the hidden beauties of the Word of God.

The silent stars twinkled softly. Far below were the lights of the city. Farther still, the waves of the Bay glistened under the rays of a crescent moon as it slid slowly toward the horizon. James felt the magic of this glorious night and was moved by it. Perhaps no more difficult task ever faces youth, than that which now confronted him.

"Marlyn," he began.

She mistook his tone. Her soft hand touched his.

He moved his own hand away. The Presence of the One Who had filled and thrilled his heart yonder in the hospital room was still with him. "Marlyn," he began once more, "I don't want to say anything to hurt you, but I'm afraid I've been a little bit too much of a coward — if you'll let me be perfectly frank with you."

"Now what?" Again her hand sought his; and again he withdrew his own.

"Marlyn, I want you to tell me the truth, do you — are you absolutely sure you love me?"

She was silent a moment. "Of course I do!"

It was his turn to be silent. He felt he was getting at the thing from the wrong angle. He wanted to shield her from as much pain as possible. Yet how to go about it —

He came directly to the point. "I may as well tell you, Marlyn, frankly and once for all, that our marriage is out of the question. I don't want to hurt you; I realize that I once asked you to be my wife, but our engagement was broken when Graig came into your life. I've been going out with you recently because I knew you were lonely and because I thought I might yet learn to love you. I hoped also to win you to Christ. But — "

"But what?"

"I have failed."

"You mean?"

"I mean that I do not and cannot love you and that I have utterly failed to win you to Christ."

"But Jimmy! Haven't I joined the church? Don't I try to be good? I've quit smoking and even going to the theater on Sundays. I believe in God. Isn't that being a Christian? I'm just as good as I know how; is there anything else I have to give up?"

"It isn't just giving up things, Marlyn, *it's taking into your life a Person — just one Person, Jesus Christ, the Son of God!*"

"Oh, but Jesus isn't the Son of God — not *really!* We're all sons of God in a sense, of course, even as He was. Dr. Feathergow says it isn't right to worship Jesus — that He didn't claim to be Deity. Only last Sunday he said the old fogey notion about being 'born again' was passing away from all intelligent religion."

James smothered a threatened explosion in his breast. "Religion! Religion! Religion! That's all I hear everywhere! Doesn't Dr. Feathergow know that we're not saved by *religion,* but by a Person! Religion never died on the cross! Religion didn't rise from the grave! Religion doesn't come into a man's heart! Religion can't save, Marlyn! The whole world is *religious* — the heathen world and all. It's Jesus — *believing* on Him, Who said 'I and My Father are one' and 'No man cometh unto the Father but by *Me*' — It's committing yourself to *Him;* trusting in *Him!* And, Marlyn — " James became suddenly tense — "you have never done that, have you?"

Marlyn shrugged. "I don't see it, James. I don't think one needs to be radical in order to be 'saved' as you call it."

Again James sighed. He knew her difficulty. She would never accept or appreciate the *Saviour* until she saw and condemned herself as a *sinner*; and as long as she continued to listen to Dr. Feathergow, she would never believe, for "Faith cometh by hearing and hearing by the Word of God"; "For how shall they hear without a preacher?"

For an hour he talked and explained to her the Way of salvation. In the end Marlyn was in tears, but in true Marlyn Favis style, she would not yield to the claims of the Man of Calvary.

While he was making his final plea she interrupted as though she had not heard what he was saying: "Why don't we get married anyway? Then if we don't like each other, we can be divorced. Everybody seems to be doing it. Come on, Jimmy!"

She slipped her arm through his and buried her face against his shoulder. It was her prettiest, most effective gesture.

His answer was to step on the starter of the car. He was through; his mind was made up. Almost savagely he turned the car around and drove back into the city. His heart thrilled with a new joy when the Sather Memorial Campanile came into view, tall and straight, glistening in the moonlight, standing in somber silhouette against the starlit sky. Another victory for the Man of Calvary!

He would find out June Darle's address. Tomorrow morning a letter would be on its way to her!

CHAPTER XXVII

June, looking out of the window of her apartment in North Denver, saw the postman coming down the street. There should be many letters this morning.

There *were* many letters. With a little gesture of gladness she seated herself at her writing desk and began to open them. A letter postmarked with Chinese characters received her first attention. It was from her parents, who for many years had labored as missionaries in China and who were now to have a much needed furlough. June's heart leaped with the anticipation of seeing them, for the letter spoke of their arrival at San Francisco. Would she meet them there? They would cable when they expected to sail, probably some time in April.

The second letter was from Harwood Glover. Another, from Mary in Nebraska, was filled with radiance and cheer. Mary and her mother were very happy together and everyone seemed kind to her. It had been a bit hard at first to live down the old memories; but with Christ all things were possible. "Help me pray, June, dear," one paragraph ran. "I have been made so happy and yet so sad. You remember Harwood Glover. What a friend he was to me in those days just after my great sorrow! I'm afraid I should have told him all about myself, for then I could have spared him the blow which sooner or later must come to him. Of course I can never marry him. He is so big and fine and has never tasted of the bitter dregs of the world. I cannot even bear to think of him, for I'm afraid I've learned to care a great deal for him. He writes that he has been called into the ministry and that he wants 'a golden-haired girl' to be his permanent 'assistant pastor.' But June, I can't tell him! And my hair isn't golden any more. I've let it return to its natural color; and I do like it better. All this has made it hard in my home town, but again, I say, 'Jesus never fails.' One can do anything with His help. I have a fine Sunday school class of

177

boys and they are the cutest little heathen ever. But I adore them all and am loved by them in return."

One letter after another June opened and read. A longing in her heart cried out for repletion and her thoughts returned to her California experiences. Many times she had chided herself for having refused James the right to correspond with her. Perhaps, through their letters, she might have won him to her Lord. Yet, she was convinced, there had been no other choice open to her. If he ever were changed, she asked herself, would he care enough to write? Would he ever again — ?

Her eyes filled with tears when she recalled the final scene in his office, when he had begged her to say "yes." That he had been sincere, she was sure; and it had required all her spiritual resources to enable her to say "no."

In the intervening months, the battle had been hard, but in it all the Omnipotent One had not forgotten her. She had even asked in prayer that He would take away her love that the struggle might be easier. Yet still her heart continued to cry out in anguish for her lover. At length she had resigned herself: there could be nothing wrong in loving him. She must only be sure that she did not rebel against the plain teachings of her Lord Who knew and understood. Perhaps through her suffering she might be a greater blessing to others bound in sorrow's chains.

So she had dared to love James with all her heart. She could not help herself. Yet she did not allow his love to dull the keen edge of the highest and most pure Love in all the universe.

She turned to the letters once more. She had not yet opened Glover's. With a sigh of wistfulness she tore open the envelope, entirely unprepared for the revelation it was to contain.

"My Dear Miss Darle:

"It seems ages since I last saw you, yet in reality it has been only a few months. How I have thanked God over and over again for allowing you to come into my life! It is to you more than to any earthly person that I am indebted for the awakening which has led me into the ministry. Day and night, almost, I study my Bible, even while I oversee things at home. Father's death meant an end to my schooling for a while at least, but walls do not a college make.

"I have been preaching recently, supplying here and there. I used to think you were a little too critical of the theology of many of our modern ministers, but a little experience last month opened my eyes, and I think I've had a sufficient jar to keep me fully awake the rest of my life.

"Of course I knew Dr. Feathergow's views were held by many pastors of various denominations and it was that knowledge which made me determine more than ever to preach only the simple, true gospel as Paul of old preached it. But I never dreamed that the apostasy was so rampant in my own beloved denomination. Mary tells me that you are writing an answer to Dr. Feathergow's book. Hurrah for you and your courage! You are the one to do it.

"Now let me tell what has recently happened to me. It was suggested that I take charge of three small country churches. I felt it was a real opportunity to try my wings as a fledgling preacher. First, of course, I must have a conference with our District Director. Well, the conference settled things! I was amazed as well as humiliated. He said he could see no future for a man with a purely conservative message today. To quote him: 'You cannot take children out of high school and college and teach them something entirely different on Sunday. Science has advanced too far in the presentation of fact to make theory in religion possible.'

"I was stunned! These words, coming from the lips of a man — a D.D. at that — who has the oversight of all the churches in our district!

"As if the great fundamental 'facts' of the Bible are mere 'theory in religion,' while those theories of our modern education which deny them are 'science' and 'fact'! Preposterous!

"Needless to say, I was denied the privilege of shepherding the three pastorless churches. But this one thing I do: *God helping me, I will preach only the gospel of historic Christianity!* Let the world run on in its blind and downward course, I am determined to snatch a few souls here and there as brands from the burning.

"My university training gives my word some weight among the young people of our town. I have a Bible class of high school students at the noon hour, four days a week and our Sunday afternoon Sunday school has grown to more than 150 in attendance. If I am refused a church in my own denomination, I still have my Bible and 'the field is the world.' Dr. Warburne of Calvary Church writes encouragingly and says to stand firm, that there are still many open doors for young men who will preach the old-fashioned gospel. He says he can find a church for me and he has recommended a thoroughly evangelical training school which I hope to enter in the fall.

"I must close. Next week I am going to Berkeley again to see my dear friend, Mr. Fownley. Thank God for him and his noble stand for Christ in these dark days. (He has been a Christian now for over three months.) After that I shall, I hope, take a little trip to Lohengren, Nebraska. You can guess why I wish to go there.

"Yours most sincerely in Christ,

"Harwood Glover."

For a long time June sat at her desk, her heart filled with praise. She had been privileged to help one young man to enter the glorious gospel ministry. What matter if he be refused a church by those in authority in his denomination? He had already discovered a Higher Authority and nothing, she felt sure, could seal his lips.

The letter touched her deeply. Was it possible that James was converted? Why had she not known it before? Why had he not told her? Yet she realized that in keeping silence he had done the only thing he could do. She dropped to her knees and prayed. When she arose a few minutes later her mind was fully made up. She would go to him and she would leave on the next train.

CHAPTER XXVIII

But June did not leave on the next train. No sooner had she risen than there was a knock at her door and a telegram was handed to her. She read the message three times before it made itself clear to her. It said

MUST BE IN BERKELEY AS SOON AS POSSIBLE WILL
HAVE ONE HOUR BETWEEN TRAINS FRIDAY 11:30 A. M.
MEET ME AT UNION STATION   (*Signed*) MARY

June decided to wait until Friday. There was also a bare possibility, she told herself, that she might yet decide not to go.

It was on the day following that she received a letter from James, telling of Blower's conversion and of his dying request. June had often wondered about the bedizened youth who had volunteered his information that day at the Bay bridge project. Her dislike for him and his insolent boldness had not robbed her of a desire to see him come to know the Lord. "I'm afraid I spoke out of season," she told herself afterward. "I needn't have talked salvation to him the first time I met him." Now she understood that the first time is sometime the last time and is, therefore, often the best time. An apparent "out of season" may become, under the leadership of the Holy Spirit, a most glorious "in season."

It was the closing words of the letter which puzzled and disturbed her. Her fingers trembled — had been trembling ever since the letter came. In irresistible waves emotions rolled over her. She did not need to wonder now if her love for James was genuine. She *knew!* Now that he was saved, the Father had permitted her love to overflow.

She read further and was stunned. Her hopes collapsed and despair clutched at her heart. In closing, the letter ran: "I am apologizing for breaking my promise to you not to write. I was constrained by a request which honor would not allow me to refuse. Marlyn accompanied me to the hospital, after which we drove to my favorite little nook far up the canyon highway, where we talked of things eternal . . ."

For June, the next few days were days of darkness and despair. She fought bravely and with all her soul, until at last she conquered. To her, the closing of the letter meant but one thing. What else could it mean? She fought back the tears and told herself that "all things work together for good to them that love God, to them that are the called according to His purpose." Marlyn's lover had returned to her, and she — June — had lost him forever.

She smiled and studied the tear-stained face in her mirror. "Romans 8:28 *is* true whether I understand it or not!" she cried. "I'll take my stand upon it, and *by His Grace I shall not be moved!*"

When Mary came on Friday, June was at the station to meet her. "We can get on as soon as the train is ready," June announced, "I am going with you, if you don't mind."

"More business?"

"Business and pleasure."

Mary studied the face of her friend. But June's expression did not permit her to say what was on the tip of her tongue.

"My mother and father are to arrive in Frisco before very long and I am going out ahead of time. It's been seven years now since I've seen them — Oh, Mary!" June exclaimed. "What adorable hair!"

"Do you like it?"

"It's beautiful — even as you are, Mary, dear."

Mary colored slightly. "Thank you, June — you know why I am what I am!"

"And it doth not yet appear what you *shall* be," June murmured softly.

"But when He shall appear, we shall be like Him."

"For we shall see Him as He is!"

"Isn't it simply grand — being a Christian, and knowing what it is really to live? How empty life was in the old days! No wonder I wanted to say good-bye to the world."

"But now?"

"I've discovered a better way to say it."

"And now you don't care whether you ever become a star or not!"

"Oh yes, I do. In fact, I *am* a star already — the kind St. Paul describes. I'm a star in your own crown, June."

"You're a gem, anyhow!"

"Speaking of the Knickerbocker, I've often wondered how you managed to get into that room so quickly. Of course you had a skeleton key, but where did you get it?"

"It was simple enough — I supposed Mother Tilden had told you. You see, the hotel manager happened to be her nephew and she had given him instructions that anything I wanted I was to have without any questions being asked. Mother Tilden and my mother were college chums years ago before Mother and Father went to China."

"It's wonderful," Mary breathed. "It all worked together so that you arrived at the hotel just in time to save me."

On the train, the conversation continued, first along one line, then another, serious or jocose, as their mood or fancy ran.

When they were nearing California, Mary talked more freely of her visit to Berkeley. "Graig left a considerable sum of money, it seems, and Dr. Warburne wanted me to come. I still haven't told mother about my being married to Graig. I couldn't stand to hurt her. I believe it would crush her completely if she knew. And since there doesn't seem to be any reason for telling her, I've kept it from her."

There was silence for some moments, each knowing the other's thoughts.

After awhile, Mary spoke again, as if to herself: "But Harwood —" Tears glistened on her eyelids.

"He will understand."

Mary stared at the green velvet seat in front of her. The clicking of the wheels over the rails kept time with her racing thoughts.

"He has a right to know," she said. "It will be my hardest task to give him up, but —" She bit her lip.

"Philippians 4:13?"

"Yes."

It was early Sunday morning when they arrived in Berkeley. They went at once to Mother Tilden's home.

California was all aglow in gorgeous early spring colors and the garden of the Tilden home was arrayed in splendor.

They attended church in the morning and listened to Dr. Warburne. The great church was packed to capacity and the message, June thought, was the most powerful she had heard him deliver. It so happened that both Fownley and Glover were present but neither June or Mary saw them.

June's thoughts kept recurring to James' letter and, of course, to Marlyn. "We drove to my favorite nook . . . and talked of things eternal." The words of his letter repeated themselves over and over in her memory. She wondered if Marlyn *could* talk of eternal things. If so, it must mean that she had made the Great Decision.

June's heart leaped with renewed interest in the sermon as she caught the words, "Green Front Book Shop." She gave the minister her undivided attention.

"One of the finest things that has ever come to our city is a truly Christian book store," Dr. Warburne declared. "It is not my purpose this morning to eulogize unduly its proprietor, but the testimony of the Green Front Book Shop is having its effect upon the people of the Bay cities. I may say that I am in hearty sympathy with Mr. James Fownley's stand against the heathenism in our modern literature. Much of our modern literature *is* heathen. Its immoral teachings, its atheistic philosophies and its worldliness are appalling.

"I recommend, I urge that every one of you join with our church in its clean literature campaign. Let us do with our anti-Christian literature, books and magazines alike, what they did in the city of Ephesus in the days of the Apostle Paul:—'*And they brought their books together and burned them before all.*' Surely one of the most terrible curses that has come upon this world is the curse of evil literature. May the thing we do next Tuesday night be duplicated throughout the length and breadth of our land and may there be a hundred thousand such bonfires before many weeks and months have passed.

"Thus may we as Christians declare to the world that our homes and our hearts shall not be besmirched with the filth and froth from the modern press. I suggest that you bring with you only one book and one magazine for burning as a public confession of your pledge to God to destroy it all. And then may you in the privacy of your own home, burn the rest of it.

"It is not the work of the church to *reform* the world. Our business — supremely so —is to proclaim the gospel that individuals may be saved *out of the world,* still to be *in it,* but not *of it.* Once a man is saved he should henceforth live a separated life. Most certainly, he should confess his Lord in a renunciation of unwholesome reading."

Just as they were leaving the church, the girls came upon Marlyn, who was walking alone after attending the Church on the Boulevard.

"And who *won't* you see?" Marlyn exclaimed exuberantly.

"Marlyn!" June gasped.

"Oh, I'm so excited!" Marlyn cried, her face aglow. "I'm going to be married tomorrow!"

June was speechless. Mary saved the day by answering: "Congratulations! Who, may we ask, is the favored gentleman?"

"Oh, you'd be smitten with astonishment!" Marlyn ejaculated. She glanced quickly at her wrist watch. "I'll have to run along now — be seeing you." She turned and hurried down the street.

For a long time neither June nor Mary spoke during their walk to Mother Tilden's home. At last Mary said softly, "My grace is sufficient for thee, June dear."

June did not reply, only the warm pressure of her hand told Mary that she had heard and appreciated.

CHAPTER XXIX

Monday morning. Today Marlyn would be married. Today James Fownley would pass forever from June's life! The morning sun rose clear and golden over the Berkeley hills and its warm rays kissed the nodding flowers and orange trees in the garden of the Tilden home. To the west, out across the Bay, the fog had lifted. Only a few, scattered, fleecy clouds floated lazily on the horizon.

Winter rains had come often this year and the brown hills had been transformed into rolling vistas of verdant green.

Today the voice of spring whispered in every breeze, sang lustily from the throats of merry songsters in the trees. The waters of a tiny, tumbling stream rippled gaily over the rocks in the far corner of the garden. Farther on the little rivulet flowed into the mirrored lake of the garden across the way. The bell-like piping of frogs joined in to make rich and full the symphony of spring.

June sat alone on the old willow seat, in her hand her small leather bound Testament. On a little table in front of her were papers, a manuscript and a few books.

For a moment she bowed her head in silence. Only her lips moved. A moment later she was leafing through the pages of a book entitled, *Christianity and the Modern Mind,* by Heironymous Feathergow. Words formed themselves on her lips and became audible in the morning air: "Dr. Feathergow, you have already been answered. In fact, your book was answered long before you ever conceived its impious blasphemies. This book — " She touched the New Testament — "just as it is — had long ago anticipated such teachings as yours."

Again June bowed her head and her words, hitherto spoken as if in soliloquy, were now addressed to a Person, the living Christ of the only God-breathed Book:

"O Christ, Thou knowest why I have written this new book."
Her hand now rested upon the bulky manuscript on the table.
"At last I am ready for it to be published. I pray that it may
find a market and that through it thousands may be turned once
more to Thy Book — that the modern mind, so called, may re-
pent and be subject to the Mind of Christ.

"And now, I pray, give me strength to bear the heavy burden
that has been given. Bless James and — Marlyn. Make their
joys complete and — and forgive me for having loved him — so
much — too much. I — I surrender once more, O precious
Christ, to Thy Will. Thy Will alone is best. Oh, — " Her voice
broke into uncontrolled sobs and she buried her face in her hands.
"Oh, I love him, I love him!" she cried, "but for Thy Sake I am
willing to give him up."

There was a step behind her.

June did not turn. She sat very quiet. The silence was tense.
For a moment there seemed to be a rest in the symphony of the
spring.

Then a voice. It was low and reverent. It spoke only one
word — tenderly: *"June!"*

Then the orchestra played on — a wild, fierce melody — dashing — terrible — a minor melody. It was James' voice. He had
come to tell her goodbye.

Slowly June turned and lifted her eyes to his, the light of despair in her own. No words escaped her lips. Only her eyes
spoke and it seemed to June as if she could read in his the joy
of a man in love. Ah, yes, why shouldn't he be happy? He was
to be married today!

Blindly, staggeringly, she rose to her feet and held out her
hand to him. "Congratulations! James — I — you'll be happy.
I — "

"I can never be happy without you, June dear." They were
standing close together. It seemed he could not resist the impulse to take her in his arms.

But he held himself in check. He must not take the initiative;
he had pledged himself never to do that. He had merely come
to greet her as an old friend. What did she mean? "Congratulations"? Ah, yes, she was referring to his faith in Christ.

"You and Marlyn must come to see me. I'll be glad — " she began.

"I don't understand."

She had removed his arm from about her waist and had stepped away from him. "Your — your — it's — it's your wedding day — isn't it?" she added, her voice more controlled.

"It could be," he said. His eyes upon hers were filled with love and misery.

"But isn't it — aren't you and Marlyn — ?"

The light broke upon him and he laughed. "Grant Weston and Marlyn Favis are to be married this afternoon," he said composedly.

Dazed, June moved toward him and held out her hands to him. The symphony of the spring burst forth once more in glorious, triumphant harmony. Her soul was thrilled and stirred until it seemed as if a mighty, joyous overture was playing in her breast.

His eyes were upon her, questioning, waiting; and a look of peace came over her features. "This is my answer, James," she whispered softly. "I am saying 'yes' to you — once for all."

He had not asked her; he had kept his vow. And he need never tell her; he could always let her think she had heard his voice. But had she not heard it? Yes, she had heard the voice of his soul and her own soul had said "yes" in glad response.

He lifted her hands and pressed them to his lips. For a moment his head remained bowed as if in worship. Then he raised his eyes to hers and saw in them once more the light of peace— the peace which had become his also, since he had come to know the Way.

"God has been very good to us, dear," he said softly.

CHAPTER XXX

A half hour later James was reminded that he had left Glover at the store. Glover, stopping in the city for a few days, had assumed his old duties in the Green Front Book Shop.

"You'll want to see our store," James said, "and I must not stay away too long or Harwood will never forgive me. He has an appointment in this very garden at eleven o'clock."

"With Mary?"

"Yes!"

They went to the store together. They paused in front of the big Bible in the display window. It was opened at the sixth chapter of second Corinthians, and it was no more than natural that two pairs of eyes, as if directed by the same Unseen Guide, should fall upon the fourteenth verse. Aloud yet softly they read it together.

"It will be a blessed yoke, I am sure," he said gently, as he slipped his arm through hers and led her inside.

It was fifteen minutes to eleven o'clock. There was no time even for greetings. "Forgive me, Harwood," James apologized. "I — here are the keys; take my car. You can just make it."

The day wore on. It was near the time for closing the store. "There's something I want you to see before we leave," she announced.

"Where did you get this?" he asked, as he glanced hastily through the neatly typed pages of a manuscript which she had handed to him from her brief case.

"From the author. You see, I am wondering if you would like to consider publishing it. It's an answer to Dr. Feathergow's *Christianity and the Modern Mind*."

James did not reply for a full minute. His face was a puzzle while his eyes fell eagerly upon the manuscript.

This paragraph met his eye: "Can we believe in the Christ of the Bible? Can we believe that He was indeed the son of God,

Who suffered and died for us, and rose again in triumph? How can we *not* believe? Have not these nineteen centuries been a witness to the truth of Christianity? To deny it we must close the door of the universe by denying the possibility of the supernatural; we must deny the only historical record — the Bible; and we must ignore the miracle that takes place in the heart of every believer. Christianity without a divine Christ is an eagle with clipped wings, it is powerless. If there be no divine Christ, there can be no accounting for Christianity."

Suddenly James faced her, admiration and pride in his look. "*You* wrote this!"

Her eyes were laughing, yet strangely sober. "With my little hatchet."

His reply was almost startling in its intensity. "O June! God has answered my prayer. Day and night I have been praying to Him that someone would be raised up to answer that book! Would I consider publishing this! *Would* I! I don't have to read it to decide. If *you* wrote it, I know it's exactly what I want."

June drew from her purse a small, white card. "There's just one condition," she said quietly, "if it meets with your approval. I'd like to have the book appear under my pseudonym." She handed him the card.

His hand trembled as he accepted it. A moment later he had her in his arms. "Darling!" he cried. "I might have known it! Only *you* could have written such a book as *Mad World*. It was that book which was used to lead me to Christ yonder in that old jail." He released her to stare at her in glad astonishment.

"But the publishers of your first book — in Denver! What will they think of your giving your new book to another publisher?"

"I am 'the publishers'," June said, her eyes laughing. "No one seemed to want *Mad World* at first, so I published it myself. That's how I've helped support Mother and Father in China."

"You have a new manager right now — both you and your books."

At that moment the door burst open and in came Mary and Harwood. Their faces were radiant and their glow was matched only by the bright red of Glover's hair.

"It's wonderful outdoors!" Mary exclaimed joyously. "The sunset is going to be gorgeous. We've been hiking up and down Strawberry Canyon all afternoon!"

"Yes!" Glover joined in, and his voice, too, was happy. "When we came down from the canyon, we followed the creek clear across the campus — beginning at the place where it comes out from under the Stadium."

THE END